Murder
By The Sea

Thanks for your support

D☆

Deni Starr

Launch Point Press
Portland, Oregon

ISBN: 978-1-63304-213-1
E-Book: 978-1-63304-214-8

FIRST EDITION

Editing: Judy Kerr, Jane Cuthbertson, Sandi Humphries
Cover: Lorelei

Published by:
Launch Point Press
Portland, Oregon
www.LaunchPointPress.com

This book is dedicated to
the whole crew at the Bertie Lou
who are always inspiring me
to kill people

Acknowledgments

My thanks to all the folks at Launch Point Press including editors Judy Kerr and Jane Cuthbertson and most especially Lori L. Lake. Thanks also to Mary and Vilik for the wonderful food at The Lavender Nest.

Deni Starr
February 2020

CHAPTER ONE

The Riverside Café

Sheets of rain pounding the road reduced visibility to twenty feet. Billie Jean "BJ" McKay found the rain a relief. It meant she was past the ice. The drive through the pass had been decidedly treacherous with black ice everywhere. Her usually surefooted VW Bug had slipped and slid all over the road. This was the first time in seven years she'd been behind the wheel of a car, and that wasn't making the drive any easier. Fortunately, traffic was so light she didn't hit anyone, which was a relief.

Once out of the pass, she took a deep breath and relaxed her grip on the wheel. According to her map, she should be somewhere close to Yew Lodge, which was right before Ocean City, Oregon. That would let her know she was close to her destination. She saw houses along the road now. The café should be along here soon. She passed the sign announcing Yew Lodge, which consisted of trailer park and bar, meaning she was close. Ah, she spotted the Texaco station and right across the street, the Riverside Café. She had arrived.

Cars were parked close to the door so BJ had to settle for a space thirty feet away. In the time it took to get from the car to the café, the rain soaked her to the skin. She paused at the door for a moment before remembering she didn't have to wait for a buzzer before going through. She just needed to open the door. She stepped inside and looked around.

The tiny café only seated about twenty-five customers at the tables and counter. The place was nearly full, which B.J. thought was odd for after eight on a Thursday night. She pulled back her hood and walked up to the counter, the heels of her cowboy boots clicking loudly on the floor. A woman working the counter looked over as BJ took a seat. In a wide mirror above the woman's head, BJ took stock of herself: slight, just over five-five, dark, curly hair, handsome features, and dark brown eyes. The lines on her face gave her a somewhat cynical expression. She wore a gray sweatshirt with a fleece-lined Levi vest over it, jeans, a red bandana around her neck, and scuffed shit-kicker cowboy boots.

BJ flipped a coffee mug on the counter right-side up.

The woman whose nametag read "Kate" handed her a menu and poured her a cup of coffee, then moved away to fill another guy's cup. After a few seconds, BJ stopped trying to get down the scalding coffee so quickly. She didn't need to try to finish it in a minute, she reminded herself. She had time now.

BJ studied the menu a moment, put it down and took a look around. Most of the folks in tonight looked local: fishermen, farmers, and lumberjacks, and only one young couple with children. Hardly surprising, being a cold night in early January. The coast didn't attract too many tourists this time of year, particularly not on a week night.

The café seemed a pleasant, homey place with a variety of menu items including beer and wine. A number of pictures of Ocean City at the turn of the century were displayed on the wall: pictures of the town, the wharf, and fishermen with their catches. BJ ordered lemon chicken and white wine. She looked Kate over discreetly when the opportunity presented itself. Her sister, Cindy, had written to BJ about Kate since Cindy had spent a lot of time at the café. In one letter she wrote, "It's hard for me to tell, you would know better than I, but I think Kate is a 'sister.'"

You certainly couldn't tell from just looking—no seven earrings in each ear—but something in her manner made BJ think Kate was lesbian. Might be wishful thinking though.

Kate was an unusually attractive forty-something woman, BJ thought, with a heart-shaped face, dark almost black hair, blue eyes, fair skin, a full sensuous mouth, and sharply cut cheekbones. She was about five inches taller than BJ with a slender frame. BJ had hoped that, given the weather and the day of the week, she'd be the only one here late in the evening and have a chance to talk to Kate alone, but it looked like Kate would have her hands full until closing.

She sipped the wine. Not bad stuff. Over seven years had passed since she'd had wine. She'd gotten drunk the night she got out of prison, but not on wine. She took another sip, letting it linger on her tongue, enjoying the taste, the luxury. Only four days out and everything seemed new to her. Drinking out of a glass instead of a plastic cup felt novel.

The chicken arrived promptly with a light salad, slice of fruit, and rice pilaf. The entire meal was excellent. Her only distraction was the need to keep looking over her shoulder. She hated having her back to the door. She also looked around at least three times to try to spot the screw on duty before reminding herself she was out. When she finished, the place was still full of people. Kate refilled a cup of coffee for the man sitting next to BJ.

"Hope you can finish that in ten minutes. I have to kick ya out at nine-thirty, you know," Kate said lightly. He took the hint and paid his tab. Two old farmers shuffled forward and paid their tabs.

BJ sipped her coffee and settled in to wait. The last customer left about ten minutes later.

"I need to be getting you out of here, soon," Kate said pleasantly.

BJ nodded. "I was hoping to have a word with you and didn't want a lot of folks around."

"What do you want to talk about?" she asked.

"I need to talk to you about Cindy Williams," BJ said, pushing the empty coffee cup away and looking intently at her host.

"How did you know Cindy?" Kate asked, her voice now reserved and cool.

BJ hesitated, "We were close."

"What do you want to know?" Kate stopped wiping down the counter and looked at her.

"I want to find out what happened."

Kate's eyes narrowed, "You're not a reporter?"

BJ shook her head. She considered saying more, but hoped Kate would do a quick read and realize they were part of the same sisterhood.

Kate studied her. "Let's get out of this place. Follow me home and we can talk there."

Visibility was nearly nonexistent. BJ almost locked bumpers a couple times while following Kate down winding, confusing backroads towards Pirate's Head and finally stopping at a house about fifteen minutes from the café. Good thing I didn't have to try and follow directions, BJ thought.

Kate unlocked the front door, and pushed it open. "Make yourself at home. I'm grabbing some wood from out back."

The house was an old, remodeled farmhouse, cozy and comfortable. BJ switched on some lights to see an interesting number of antique pieces: a cherrywood wine table, elegantly carved walnut sewing cabinet, and pie-crust card table set against beach décor of Japanese glass floats, seashells, and an artistic arrangement of fishing net. BJ's sister had been an antiques dealer. She wondered if Cindy had had anything to do with Kate's antiques. She pulled off her boots, vest, and damp sweatshirt deciding the initials OWCF on her t-shirt weren't exactly self-explanatory.

BJ went over to the bookshelf and looked at the selection. Certainly were some revealing works. She found *Gynecology, Pure Lust, Going Out of Our Minds,* and mysteries by Lori Lake, Katherine Forrest, and Jessie Chandler.

Kate entered the room with an armful of wood. "Find something you wanted to read?"

"I think I've read everything here."

"I see you made yourself at home."

"Yeah, I did." BJ took a seat near the fireplace.

Kate quickly got the fire going.

BJ asked, "Why is there a glass of water on the mantel?"

"To invite the Fire Fairies in to dance so the fire will start. Would you like a brandy?" Kate asked as the flames grew and lit the room.

"I would love a brandy."

Kate took two snifters down from a shelf on the buffet, took a bottle from it and poured each of them a drink.

"Hmmm, damn fine stuff," BJ said, inhaling the aroma.

Kate sat down on the floor cross-legged a few feet away from where BJ was rocking in the ancient rocking chair. BJ watched the light from the fireplace play over Kate's face, highlighting her high cheekbones, then in an instant, leaving her face in darkness creating the illusion that Kate was fading in and out of the shadows, more a phantom than a presence.

"How well did you know Cindy?" Kate asked.

"She was my sister." BJ took another sip, looking over the top of her glass to study Kate's expression.

Kate raised her eyebrows quizzically. "You'll pardon me for not noticing the family resemblance."

"Cindy was my half-sister. We had different fathers." BJ took another drink, the smooth brandy causing her stomach to warm.

"Which explains why she's black and you're not."

"She's biracial." BJ reached into the back pocket of her jeans and pulled out her wallet which contained a set of snapshots in a plastic holder. She handed Kate pictures of her with Cindy at various ages starting at four and six, with the most recent one of BJ in a tuxedo standing behind Cindy who wore a wedding gown.

"Who was older?" Kate asked.

"I was."

Kate looked over the photos carefully, studying each one, finally handing them back to BJ who returned them to her wallet and tucked it back in her pocket.

"What are you here for?"

"I came to wrap things up. Get her stuff, sell the house, all that."

"You took your time getting here. Cindy was murdered nine months ago and you're just now showing up? What have you been doing?"

"Time."

"What?"

"I've been doing time. The initials on my shirt stand for Oregon Women's Correctional Facility."

Kate looked at her blankly for a moment. Regaining her composure, she asked, "What were you in for?"

"I was in for four years, ninety-six days, and sixteen hours."

"That's not what I meant."

"I know what you meant."

Kate looked at her and took a sip of brandy. Finally, she said, "What did you want to ask me about?"

"I want to know what happened to Cindy. I know you and she knew each other, so I thought I'd start with you."

Kate shook her head. "I have no idea. I don't know any more than what I've read in the papers. When the sheriff has come by the café, he's just said they're working on some leads."

"He's a regular at the café?"

"Everyone in town is. Have you tried contacting him?" She got up, refilled both snifters with more brandy, and sat down again.

"He won't give me the time of day. I wrote him as soon as I found out, but you don't get a lot of respect when your return address is the State Prison."

"So, you don't know anything about it at all?"

"I read a three-inch column in *The Oregonian*, and that's all I know. Her uncle on her father's side made all the arrangements after her death." BJ didn't say anything more on that subject. She knew if she got started on how frustrating, painful, nearly intolerable it had been to know practically nothing and not be able to get information from anyone, she wouldn't be able to shut up about it. It was so hard to even mention it without wanting to throw her glass against the wall and smash it. Instead, she took another sip of brandy and tried to slow her heartbeat, keep her voice even.

Kate said, "Our local paper gave it a lot of ink. Even so, no one here knows much of anything, unless the sheriff does. She was found first thing in the morning by some guy out walking his dog on the beach. Actually, the dog found her up above the dune grass by a warehouse. She'd been strangled."

"I did know she'd been . . . strangled." BJ said, almost unable to say the word.

"I think they had a suspect, but it didn't pan out, don't remember why not. I think that's all anyone knows. If law enforcement has some theory on motive, they're not sharing."

"How would I get back issues of the local paper?"

"Ocean City Herald morgue. They keep old issues going back forever. Didn't your family tell you anything?" Kate asked looking puzzled.

"I don't have much by way of family anymore. I have an aunt in Phoenix that I haven't talked to in twenty-five years."

"Didn't Cindy's family tell you anything?"

"I was in prison. They weren't talking to me."

"The Oregonian didn't have anything?" Kate pursued, now looking sympathetic.

"That's where I found the three-inch article." BJ gripped the handrest of the chair, using muscle tension to try to keep her anger at bay.

"The Herald had a lot more than that," Kate offered helpfully.

"Guess I'll start there." BJ needed to change the subject—and fast—before she started breaking up the furniture. "By the way, nice little place you have here."

"Thanks. I inherited it from my father. He and my mother retired here after he left the Army. My Aunt Jane was running the café. My parents came down and helped out with the business, then when Jane retired, they took it over."

"Did Jane pass away?"

"No, she and her lover, Mabel, are living in a retirement home in Salem."

BJ smiled a wry smile. "You know, I've always been told that the phrase 'living in Salem' was a contradiction in terms and the phrase 'retiring to Salem' was redundant."

"Not my choice."

"So, you came out here to be with your family?"

"No. My parents died within two months of each other, heart attack and then stroke. I'd recently divorced my husband and needed to start over somewhere with something, so I came down here after inheriting the house and business."

BJ released her death grip on the chair. The anger was fading, and she was starting to feel comfortably relaxed, a combination of the warm fire and brandy. She had been so angry so often after Cindy's death, that the pain now came and went pretty quickly. It was so pleasant to sit here, listening to the rain on the roof, looking at the fire, talking to this beautiful woman.

"You live here by yourself?" BJ asked.

"Mostly. I have a friend in Portland who comes down and stays as often as her job allows, but lately the visits have been few and far between." Kate frowned again.

That gave BJ the impression the friend in Portland had likely found a new friend.

"You didn't have a career going in Portland when you got a divorce?"

"No. Clyde and I were both in the Army. I joined after high school since there wasn't money for college. You get more pay and better perks in the service if you're married."

"You married a man?" BJ quizzed, raising her eyebrows.

Kate shrugged. "I knew three days after the wedding I'd made a mistake, but it took me eight years to admit it. I'd have admitted it a lot sooner, but Clyde was usually on a tour of duty and out of the country. That left me on base by myself. And you?"

"Oh, that's a mistake I haven't made yet. A few serious involvements, but never married."

"What did you do before you did time?"

"I do leatherwork, saddles mostly."

"Really? I don't know many saddle makers."

"The field is hard to get into. They don't teach it in community colleges. You find someone already in the trade and have her teach you. My teacher had a lot of connections with rodeo people, so I got to make a lot of the fancy parade-style silver saddles. I do some other stuff now and then, belts, and when I need a quick turn-over in merchandise, holsters and rifle scabbards."

"Did you work in like a factory, or shop, or what?"

"I turned my garage into a workshop and worked from there. The people who wanted parade saddles would get in touch with me. When things were slow, I'd turn out the holsters and scabbards and sell those to local gun shops."

"Know a lot about guns?"

"Nope. Just a lot about leather."

"And you liked it?"

"It pays pretty well, satisfies my creative instincts and saves me from having to work with a lot of geeks."

"Did you have to learn a trade when you were in prison?"

"I had to stay busy, but I didn't have to learn a trade. They had classes and stuff, but they're mostly to help people get their GEDs. How about yourself? Where'd you learn to cook?"

"Self-taught. Most people thought I learned in the Army, but I never once had to do KP. Thank goddess, or I'd probably hate my job now. I was in the unit's journalism department."

"Did you get background in that while you were in high school?" BJ asked.

"Oh, some. I've always been a good writer. Actually, I was assigned to the journalism department after having to complete a five-hundred-word essay on the importance of saluting a superior officer."

BJ guessed there was a pretty good story in back of that one. "Do you like running the café?"

"It pays pretty well, satisfies my creative instincts, and I don't have to work with a lot of geeks," Kate said with a smile.

"Must be getting on pretty late." BJ set her snifter on a nearby table and checked her watch.

"Where are you staying?" Kate remained seated on the floor.

"Dunno. I thought I'd cruise into town and find a cheap motel."

"Not a lot of money?

"I have some. My landlady sold everything I owned after I went to jail. Fortunately, she sent me the money, most of which I'd had in a savings account. Also, fortunately, my VW was still waiting for me when I got out. She'd put it in her garage so—new battery, air in the tires, and it was up and running. Bugs don't die. You have to kill them.

"Aren't they supposed to give you ten dollars and a new suit?"

"No new suit, but I did get a bus ticket to make sure I left town."

"Well, if you wouldn't mind a couch, you're welcome to stay here. It's a bit late to try to find your way to town."

"Thanks. I'd appreciate it."

Kate set about making up the couch, and BJ went in to take a bath. The bathroom was pleasantly decorated in greens and yellow with plants and fragrant soaps. She loved bathtubs. Prison had only showers. She spent nearly seven years taking showers. Soaking in a tub was a wonderful luxury. She stripped off her still slightly damp jeans and T-shirt and climbed into the steaming water.

Getting into the tub, her eye fell on the jagged scar running along the inside of her arm. Amazing what a creative person could turn into a weapon. BJ knew that she'd been awfully lucky to catch that shiv with her arm instead of having it buried in her chest.

A skylight over the bath let her see the rain splashing against glass. She closed her eyes and relaxed. The brandy was making her feel warm and lazy. She was pleased to have found such a cozy harbor in the storm.

Of course, that didn't make her forget why she was there. Back when she'd found out about Cindy's death, she had felt, powerfully and irrationally, that it couldn't be true, that if she could only leave prison and come down to the coast, she could straighten the whole thing out and Cindy would be alive again. She contacted her former lawyer and asked him to do everything he could to get her out early, since she had only nine months to go on her sentence. He wasn't able to do anything for her, and she wasn't even allowed a temporary pass to attend Cindy's funeral. Since their mother had died and BJ had no other family members, the only relatives the women had in common were Cindy's family. But they refused to have anything to do with BJ after her incarceration.

The first few days after BJ got the news, she created such a fuss that her jailers hauled her down to the prison psychiatrist who threatened to drug and confine her to a bed. The threat was enough to make BJ less frantic, but days went by before she could eat again and months before she stopped her maniacal pacing. After nine months, she got used to having this unremitting anguish in her life, but it still caused her intense pain.

The torment abated considerably after her release because, even if Cindy's death could not be changed, BJ could still do something in response besides pace a tiny cell that wasn't much bigger than a walk-in closet.

But tonight, she thought, she could give herself some time off from her hurt and feel good about where she was and happy to be better.

The couch proved to be comfortable, and she lay contentedly watching the fire die and listening to the rain drum on the roof, slowly drifting off to sleep.

BJ woke up automatically at six-thirty, rise-and-shine time in the pen. She got up and wandered into the kitchen. Kate had left a pot of coffee and some Danish out with a note saying she was at the café, and would BJ please lock the door when she left.

BJ got some fresh clothes from the car, showered, had another cup of coffee and headed into town. She stopped at the café to get a full breakfast. Bacon and eggs still seemed incredible to her. Prison offered the choice of hot cereal or cold cereal. Seven years, hot cereal or cold cereal. The café was packed, but she snagged the last seat at the counter. Kate gave her a smile and a cup of coffee.

"Did you sleep all right?" Kate asked, passing over some cream.

"Slept great," B.J. said, returning Kate's smile. "Best night's sleep I've had in a long time."

"You're up awful early."

"Conditioning. Damn, but you make a good cup of coffee."

"Keeps people coming back."

"I meant at your house."

"So did I. What can I get you for breakfast?"

"Bacon, scrambled eggs, hash-browns, toast, and milk, please."

"Is that all?"

"Add some pork chops with that." BJ winked.

"Coming right up."

BJ wolfed down her food, habit making her think she had a short time to eat. She looked at the other diners eating sausage, benedicts, fried razor clams, and other wonders BJ hadn't had in years, and thought about ordering some, but had to acknowledge she'd had enough for one meal. It was simply going to take time to catch up on everything she had missed out on while in stir. Leaving cash on the counter, she got back into her car and headed into town.

BJ remembered visiting Ocean City with her family when she was a child. She was amazed that some of the old restaurants and coffee shops were still in business over thirty years later. There were also the kite shops, touristy t-shirt shops, shell shops, and bookstores that'd she'd loved as a kid. Now there were Starbuck drive-throughs, shops advertising blown glass artistry and signs for brew pubs but it hadn't lost the character of a sleepy small beach town. She guessed most of the residential growth was away from the ocean front which was still hotels and beach cottages. She might have been here in the Sixties for all that there was any traffic going down the main strip into town, but she reminded herself that it was early on a weekday in January. It was probably much different on the weekends in summer.

She located the city newspaper after some trouble with the GPS app on her phone, which kept wanting to send her the wrong way down one-way streets, but eventually tracked it down. She went up to a friendly-looking middle-aged woman who appeared to act as receptionist and asked about seeing back issues. She didn't introduce herself or explain. She was directed to the basement where another friendly woman showed her where the most recent back issues were, explaining that they were kept filed by date in the large file cabinets going back twelve months, and that anything older was now on microfiche.

BJ was a little surprised that no one wanted to see her ID or get an explanation of what she was looking for, but then, how valuable were old newspapers whose content was on computers systems anyway? Clearly, they weren't worried about someone stealing them, or even misfiling them. Before leaving, the woman gestured to a cash operated copy machine against one wall and was told help would be available to download stories from computers if BJ had any trouble making copies. Then she was left to her own devices.

The woman was pleasant and helpful. She didn't seem to feel any compulsion to quiz her visitor. BJ quickly found the first article on the murder and the next ones after. She found lengthy articles in the two weeks following her sister's death, but they thinned out, finally disappearing altogether.

"Local Women Found Strangled" the headlines blared. Common headlines, BJ thought. You see something like it every day. How odd when it was your family. She copied the articles but didn't read them.

She didn't feel able to do that in pubic, where someone might walk in and find her crying over the copies.

When she got what she needed, BJ left the newspaper office and decided to go see Cindy's house. Cindy moved out to the coast when her husband, who worked for a timber company, was transferred to a mill near Ocean City. They divorced a few years later but by then Cindy had become attached to the coast, and since Bill's company transferred him back to the valley, she decided to stay on. She got a job with Bingham Antiques, *the* prestigious antique store on the coast. While Bingham's catered somewhat to tourists, they were not a "tourist" shop. They sold to the wealthier local family businesses wanting atmosphere and opulence and to a lot of shops in Portland and Seattle.

From their long, frequent phone calls, BJ knew Cindy spent weekdays in the shop, chatting with fellow enthusiasts about the wares, and her weekends cruising the local garage sales, estate sales, and barn sales for "finds." She called it treasure hunting and enjoyed it immensely. She'd gotten on reasonably well with the senior partners of the store and with the sales clerks. Her position was somewhere in the middle. She sold at the store as a clerk, but she was also entrusted with buying, something only the two partners were allowed to do. BJ knew Cindy's ambition was to save up enough money to open a store of her own.

"I like the people I work with," she'd written BJ, "but my favorite colleague is Mitch Quigley, who owns the store across the street from ours. There are six of us in the same two-block stretch of downtown. We get all the antique hunters down to our end of town. Mitch sells more knick-knacky stuff than we do, but he also has quite a passion for Oriental pieces and picks up some great pieces from time to time. He gets most of it from estate sales of men who went to the Orient during the war. He's a 'brother,' but doesn't act like one unless he has customers. They almost expect antique dealers to be gay. He has a wonderful African-American lover named Dennis who works for the county. We don't run into much prejudice here. The townspeople consider blacks and gays to be exotics who add some color to the landscape. I'm sure they would feel differently if we black folk weren't such a minority. The locals feel so threatened by the Hispanic migrant workers that they consider anyone who isn't Hispanic to be an honorary white. I can't make up my mind to feel amused or insulted. Anyway, the locals are mostly tolerant and almost expect me to get involved with another white man. I've even been set up on a few blind dates. No one interesting, yet."

Cindy had written that letter shortly after her divorce.

It took BJ longer to find Cindy's house than it had to find the newspaper office, mostly because her GPS kept wanting to send her to Kiev, but she found it. In keeping with Cindy's taste for antiques, the house was from the last century, a miniature Victorian set back in the hills, slightly inland from the city, standing on a quarter acre of land bordered by two-hundred-foot-tall old growth firs, making it seem secluded. BJ parked her car in the driveway and got out.

Cindy had sent her a picture after she'd bought it two years ago, but she'd never been here. BJ inspected the premises from the outside and found no signs of vandalism or violence. The house seemed quiet and restful. The only reminder of violence was the official police seal on the door. BJ looked through the front porch's bay window. The furniture seemed all there, as far she could tell. Nothing seemed disturbed. She found the extra key Cindy had hidden and put it in her pocket. She didn't go in. She needed police permission first. She figured the area was no longer being preserved as evidence after this long a period of time, and there was no yellow crime scene tape anywhere, but a seal on the door posted a notice of no entry.

Technically she owned the house. While still in prison, BJ was contacted by a lawyer who had drafted Cindy's will informing her she was both the sole heir and executor. He had referred her to an attorney in Portland. BJ had hired the Portland lawyer by letter, and right before coming to the coast, had gotten papers from his office indicating she owned the estate.

BJ tried the front door and found it locked. She went to the back door to make sure the house was secured, and finding everything locked up, went back to the car and left. The sheriff's office was in Westport, a thirty-minute drive down the coast. She got there slightly after twelve, deciding to have lunch to fortify herself for a meeting with the Sheriff. She pulled over at a modest looking place called The Crab Cooker, and walked in. This time she remembered to open the door, but then she took a seat that put her back to the wall so no one could get behind her. Not letting anyone come up behind her had become a way of life over the last seven years. It was a jail thing.

A few minutes after she'd sat down, a pretty, Hispanic young woman came over to take her order. She tried hard not to stare at the woman's luxuriant black hair and dark brown eyes. BJ was taken aback by seeing so many people who looked, so, so *normal*. She thought it odd to see a woman who had healthy skin tone, instead of prison pallor, wearing make-up, dressed neatly, and looking healthy.

She ordered clam chowder and a shrimp salad. She liked seafood, definitely a change from what she was used to. They never got seafood in prison. She also ordered the marionberry pie with ice cream, and finished her coffee before feeling ready to leave. She paid her tab, left a generous tip, and went to find the sheriff's office.

Sheriff Carstairs wasn't what she had pictured. She had an image in her mind of some pot-bellied, greasy-haired yokel out of an episode of *Dukes of Hazzard*. Sheriff Carstairs was over six feet tall and lean. His uniform was ironed crisply and he wore a Rolex watch. His hair was so long it touched the collar of his shirt and covered his ears. Despite the hair, he had a military bearing BJ judged to be the result of time in the military. He had steely blue eyes and lines around his mouth that looked like he spent a lot of time frowning. He did not greet BJ with any form of enthusiasm. After she stated her business, he acted like if he ignored her long enough, she would leave. However, she camped in a chair, prepared to stay, and eventually he got around to having someone issue her a document clearing the seal and allowing her entry into the house.

"You aren't planning to stay here, are you?" he asked coldly.

"I might. What's it to you?"

"We don't like your kind around here."

"Oh? What kind is my kind?"

"Convicts. And don't give me your excuse for your crime."

"I wasn't going to. Everybody I did time with had an excuse and I didn't believe theirs. I don't assume you'd believe mine. Besides, I don't see any reason to excuse myself to you." She tucked the papers in her pocket and departed.

Not someone who got elected on his congeniality, she thought. If this was the guy to give her information on the investigation of Cindy's death, she wasn't going to get much. She wondered if he knew what she'd been in for, or just despised ex-cons in general.

She got back to Ocean City around six. Time again for a meal, she thought. This bit about being able to eat whenever it seemed reasonable, as opposed to only at strictly enforced hours, was a novelty to BJ. She loved it. She drove north through town and stopped at the Riverside Café again. Once again, the place was packed. She got one of two seats left at the counter.

"How'd things go?" Kate asked, pouring her a of cup of coffee.

"They went. Can't say I had a good time."

"Where are you staying?"

"I haven't decided. I'll move into Cindy's place but I don't want to do that tonight. I'd guess all the utilities are off. I'll drive back into town and find a place."

Kate got coffee to the other customers and came back to take her order. BJ decided to go with the blackened shark. She found the meal was as good as the one last night. The food here was excellent.

Kate left a tab that said 'on the house' and handed her a key. "Leave the light on for me," she said.

"Trusting soul, aren't you?"

"l liked your sister. I liked her a lot."

"Thanks."

BJ drove out to the house and once in, got a fire going. She brought in her bag, and some food she had bought earlier. After putting a few things away, she opened a bottle of red wine she'd picked up in town, found a glass, got settled, and started to read the copies of the news articles she had gotten. "Local Woman Found Strangled" was the first headline.

Cindy Williams, a local resident, was found dead outside the Kalberer warehouse. The body was found at five a.m. by Mr. George Rusk, who was jogging in the area with his dog. The cause of death was determined to be strangulation according to Melissa Cody, spokesperson for the Ocean County Sheriff's department. The police currently have no leads in the case. Ms. Williams, originally from Portland, had resided in Ocean City for the past four years and worked as a salesclerk for the Bingham Antique Establishment.

"Everyone here is so shocked. We can't imagine how this happened," said Jim Marsh, Ms. Williams's supervisor. "She was well-liked by everyone at the store and was one of our best employees." When asked if he had any theories on the case, he indicated he assumed an outsider passing through town committed the murder.

The sheriff's office is conducting an investigation of the matter. Asked if the homicide might be sexual in nature, the sheriff indicated it was too early to tell. The body was found fully clothed. The sheriff would not say if she was murdered at the site where she was found or somewhere else. Anyone having any knowledge of the event or who saw anything unusual is asked to report it immediately to the homicide division of the Sheriff's office.

The following day, the headline was for a feature story, "Murder Victim from Patriotic Family."

Ms. Cindy Williams, whose fully clothed body was found yesterday morning at five a.m., came from a family with a long history of service to this country. Her father, Major Reeves Williams was a highly decorated veteran of the Vietnam War, winning a bronze star and purple heart. Her two uncles, Roger and Roosevelt Williams, also served in the war and both won purple hearts, and Roger Williams was awarded a bronze star. Her third uncle, Richard Williams, was killed in action in Vietnam. Shortly after returning from Vietnam, Major Williams married Maureen McKay, who had a two-year-old child from a previous marriage. The couple divorced five years later and Major Williams retained custody of Cindy, then five years old.

According to her family, Cindy was a sweet child who was well-liked in her neighborhood. "She was accepted by everyone. There wasn't anyone who didn't like her," said Mrs. Roger Williams. Ms. Williams had attended Roosevelt High School and was on the annual Rose Festival Rose Court her senior year. She attended the University of Washington in Seattle majoring in communications. She was married two days before graduation to John Towerson, also of Seattle. The marriage was annulled after six months. Later she married Bill Weathers. The couple arrived in Ocean City six years ago and were well-liked. Mr. Weathers was transferred to Silver Creek Falls, and the couple was divorced. Ms. Williams had her maiden name restored and continued to live in Ocean City. She was employed as a store manager for Bingham Antiques for the last four years.

The County Sheriff currently has no updates regarding her murder. Anyone with information is requested to please come forward immediately by contacting the County Sheriff at Westport.

An obituary and funeral notice repeated the same general information.

The third article was dated two weeks later and headed "Suspect Detained in Murder Case." A man by the name of Steven Garrick, arrested in connection with a burglary, was identified as a suspect in a local rape case. However, he was soon cleared of being involved in Cindy's murder. At the time Cindy died, he was in jail in Tillamook. News of his release came in a short article two days after the news of his arrest.

About a week after Garrick's release, another article mentioned Cindy's murder and indicated two women hikers were found dead in a remote area five miles off a popular hiking trail. The bodies had been decomposing for months. Some speculated these deaths might have some relationship to Cindy's, but the sheriff's office declined to say whether or not evidence existed linking the two occurrences. Two months later, the last article on Cindy's murder appeared, a brief interview with Sheriff Carstairs indicating most of the leads came to dead ends. No evidence of sexual assault was found.

BJ noted the names of the three different reporters who'd written the articles in case she could get more information from them. She folded the papers and put them away. She put some more logs on the fire and poured herself another glass of wine.

It was starting to sink in that Cindy was gone. Ten times a day BJ wanted to pick up the phone and call Cindy, only to remember she couldn't. She often dreamed she was seeing Cindy, and then remember and wake up crying. Nine months now, and the grief had not subsided. They'd been close as children in spite of the divorce.

Cindy's father filed for divorce when BJ was seven and Cindy was five. He filed for custody, and a protracted court fight occurred, neither parent willing to lose. The judge placed Cindy with her father as a show of willingness to accept "father's rights" in spite of the violence it did to Cindy and BJ's relationship. Weathers remarried shortly afterwards, and Cindy then had a stepmother. Fortunately, neither family left Portland, and they lived only twenty minutes apart.

Cindy came to visit every other weekend and spent half the summer with BJ and their mother. They split major holidays, and BJ visited with Cindy then. She was always welcome to come over and spend a weekend with her. At first, Cindy's black relatives were amused by BJ, and by their community's reaction to introducing BJ as a relative. But the novelty of that soon wore off, and she was just another white kid from the west side.

Her black step-relations treated her politely, and her aunt D'Norgia had always been her favorite adult, next to her mother. When BJ turned fourteen, she selected Roosevelt High School, knowing Cindy would be attending it in two years. They had a peculiar relationship with one another's peers. BJ insisted Cindy be accepted even though she was black, and Cindy insisted that BJ be accepted even though she was gay. In September of her senior year, which was Cindy's sophomore year, an incident cemented their relationship and permanently endeared BJ to Cindy's relatives.

Cindy was waiting at her locker for BJ when a senior boy, the white quarterback of the football team, made a pass at Cindy. She politely indicated she was not interested. He grabbed her, ripped open her shirt, and forced her back against the wall . . . and then BJ arrived. From behind, BJ planted the top of a shit-kicker boot between the boy's legs with all the power she could muster. He doubled over. She grabbed him by the hair, swung him against the wall, and knocked out half of his teeth with her knee.

The white boys were outraged that a dyke had beaten up one of their own. The black community was outraged that a white boy had attacked a black girl. The gay community was outraged that a lesbian was being singled out for harassment. The women's community was outraged that the boy had received a slap on the wrist because he was a member of the football team. The adults were so busy with their own particular grudge and with responding to conflicting opinions, that Cindy and BJ soon became forgotten parts of the controversy. BJ was the hero of her step-relatives, and Cindy was respected for her unswerving loyalty to her sister in the subsequent brouhaha. The event had brought the fact of BJ's existence to the attention of Sara, another senior and another dyke, who became BJ's first real lover.

The sisters became inseparable. Even with their different life paths, they stayed close.

Cindy visited her regularly at the jail and had attended every day of court proceedings. She traveled to Salem once a month to visit after BJ was convicted.

"If I hadn't been in the pen, this wouldn't have happened." BJ muttered to herself, again.

The door rattled and Kate came in. "Don't you want some light on in here?" she asked, flipping on the overhead lights in the kitchen and the living room.

"Hmm? Oh, I'm sorry. I should have left the porch lights on for you." BJ had lost all sense of time and place as she focused on reading about the murder. She hadn't noticed that other than her reading lamp, she was sitting in a dark house.

"How was your day?" Kate asked, shedding her jacket.

"Depressing. You want a glass of wine?"

"Yeah, sure. What have you got?"

"Pinot Noir."

"Sure."

BJ got up and poured Kate a glass and re-filled her own. Kate took hers and plopped down in a nearby chair. "Did you get what you wanted from the newspaper?"

BJ nodded. "What there was, yeah."

"Must be hard to read through all that," Kate sympathized, taking a sip of her wine.

"Hard isn't the word."

"You got plans for tomorrow?"

"I'm going to move into her house and get the utilities back on."

"Who does the house belong to now?" Kate sat in a chair near the fire.

"Me. She left a will giving me her estate."

"Let me know if I can do anything."

"Thanks."

They sat for a while in companionable silence until Kate picked up the bottle of wine, poured herself more, and refilled BJ's glass. BJ looked up and smiled at this truly beautiful woman. Too bad she was too depressed to care. Still, she felt pleased to be where she was and to have the company. Kate built up the fire and returned to her chair, sipping her wine and studying BJ.

"Do you plan on staying in Ocean City?"

"Dunno. My work lets me set up shop anywhere. I can take orders for saddles from all over the country. I've still got all my tools. It'd be easy to set up over at Cindy's place. I'm not sure I'm into small-town life though. I'm more a big city person. I've always enjoyed a bigger women's community."

"Maybe you should give it a try."

"Maybe I should. I love the ocean."

"I should let you in on a secret about the ocean, though," Kate whispered conspiratorially.

"What?"

"It never stops making that noise."

BJ laughed.

BJ fixed herself breakfast the next morning, did the dishes, made up the couch, left a thank you note and the last of the wine, then drove back to Cindy's house in Ocean City. The sheriff's No Entry warning was still on the front door. BJ pulled it down and went inside. The house was unnaturally quiet. It seemed to be holding its breath, waiting for something.

She went from room to room, looking over the furniture and knickknacks. Some things she recognized from Cindy's childhood, but most of them were things Cindy must have bought after she'd moved to the coast. After she carefully examined each room, she left to go in to town and talk in person with the various utilities. She doubted she could get anything turned on without actually showing her executor documents proving she had the right to the house and writing a check for a deposit. The lawyer who drafted Cindy's will had prepared the necessary documents to transfer funds to BJ's prison account before BJ was released, so that had all been in place upon her release.

She wrangled with various water, gas, and electrical officials, then went grocery shopping and returned to the house. After putting things away, she went through the house even more carefully, looking for any little thing that was odd or out of place. Everything seemed in order. She could tell the police had gone through things, but had put them back, leaving the house as they'd found it. Everything looked ready for occupancy.

Cindy's checkbook was on a table by the front door. Upstairs her clothes were flung in the direction of the laundry hamper. Her makeup lay scattered around the bathroom sink. The place looked as if she were going to walk in any minute. BJ would pick something up, look at it, and put it back down. She didn't change anything. She found a picture of herself on the bureau in the bedroom. She went back downstairs, got a fire started to get some heat going. She still had no electricity, so she lit some of Cindy's antique oil lamps for light and went over to Cindy's bookshelves to look through them. In addition to general reading topics, Cindy had two dozen books and magazines on antiques and a half dozen or so about the coast, including local hikes, shipwrecks, and local ghosts.

BJ looked through Cindy's huge roll-top oak desk that took up most of one wall of the living room. The desk was too big for Cindy's small office, not to mention being a beautiful antique that Cindy no doubt wanted guests to see. BJ lifted the rolltop and sat down to take a look in the various cubbyholes and drawers. Cindy had neatly filed and tucked away her credit card and bank statements for the last several months. BJ glanced through the paper copies. She found bank transfers paying for utilities, gas, and groceries, and smaller credit card and check amounts to individuals listed as "Sales." BJ assumed the purchases were for things Cindy had picked up at garage sales and estate sales. None of the amounts were all that much. The grocery bill was the largest.

In another cubbyhole of the desk was a packet of letters, held together with rubber bands. BJ recognized these as ones she'd written from prison. Her name and SID—Security ID—number were on the return address space on the envelopes. She was reluctant to touch the letters, as if the tangible reminder of her incarceration could somehow transport her back, as if when she touched them, she'd wake up and find herself back in her cell. She knew she needed to get past those feelings, and it wouldn't be easy. She wasn't going to re-read the letters, she told herself. She was just checking the desk.

She glanced through the pack to make sure there was nothing else and put them back. She sighed with relief, and went on with her search.

One cubbyhole held sealing wax and a stamp that Cindy always used to seal her envelopes. Another cubbyhole held pleas for charitable donations and a list of various groups, made out in Cindy's handwriting, which noted contributions with the date and amount.

Tucked between some bills she found a registered letter. BJ opened it to find a short scrawl on letterhead:

> RE: Your Inquiries
> 1899 10 Ruble Note – promising, and ornamental
> egg definitely of good provenance and value.
> Hopping a plane to Georgia – more later,
> Lucy

BJ wondered what that was a about. She opened one of the desk drawers and found another bundle of letters. This was a more random assortment. The first several were from Cindy's ex-husband Bill, the correspondence having to do with Bill not paying a marital debt as per the divorce decree, which he had seemed reluctant to do. That schmuck, BJ thought to herself.

Several letters were from a woman in Portland, who, from the content of the letters, BJ guessed was an interior designer. Her name was Lynn Langford and it seemed she did business with Cindy on friendly terms. The letters were more gossip and folksy with only a few passing references to purchases. Another bundle was an odd assortment of letters from Cindy's family. Her three aunts had written some notes, and one long letter was from her uncle Roger. Nothing but family news. Last was a letter from a Mister Edward West inquiring about the purchase of a sea chest. BJ thought it a bit odd. The letter seemed a pure business correspondence, but Cindy didn't have any other business letters in her desk.

There was no laptop on the desk. BJ assumed the police must have taken it as evidence since that was standard procedure in all criminal cases these days. It would probably stay in police custody as long as the case was still open, so she would have to content herself with learning what she could from the old-fashioned snail-mail correspondence. She assumed Cindy had a computer at work, but she also knew Cindy had still preferred to keep most of her notes and personal records in hard-copy, the result of having a laptop die some years ago and wipe out all the data. BJ knew Cindy hadn't adjusted to doing financial transactions online, instead keeping paper records of her banking and credit card statements, just an old-fashioned girl.

BJ scanned the drawers. She found stationary, notepads, stamps, pens, flyers on community events, note sheets on antique prices, a few mail-order catalogues for clothes, and a collection of newspaper clippings from various small, local newspapers up and down the coast. All of these were in reference to estate sales. The names of the agencies responsible for the sales were circled in red ink.

In another drawer she found a ledger with a listing of purchases inside. Neatly entered in Cindy's elegant script was the date, a description of the item, a notation as to where it was purchased, the amount paid for it, and whether it was for the shop or herself. A separate notation recorded whether or not she had fronted the money for a shop item, and when the shop had reimbursed her. BJ counted a dozen items Cindy had picked up for the shop but not been paid for. BJ needed to see if those items were still here, or if they'd been turned over to the shop, and if so, she needed to be reimbursed.

The last item of interest in the desk was an address book. BJ recognized most of the names in it, but a half dozen she didn't know. Something else to check out, she thought, putting the book back.

Finished with the desk, BJ wandered around the house, not looking for anything in particular, just taking it in. The dining and living room were neat, attractively furnished and relatively clean considering how much time had passed with the house shut. Other than some dust, the kitchen was spotless. The office area was cluttered with a collection of bric-a-brac, books, magazines, and boxes. She sat down and browsed through the stack of magazines and books on the table. One was a magazine on Victoria, BC, another on early American furniture, one on antique glassware, another for antique paintings, and antiques from Russia. BJ noticed they were all subscription magazines except for the Russian one which looked brand new, as if it had been purchased from a news stand recently; however, from the date on the cover, it was almost a year old.

The house was still cold. The gas company would send someone out tomorrow to get her furnace going. In the meantime, she had to rely on the fireplace. She heaped more logs on it, then toured the house to make sure all the windows were closed and locked.

Cindy was killed in May, back when she might have had windows open. BJ discovered that all the windows were locked. Not only were they locked, but the locks looked brand new. BJ checked the three doors to the house. The front door lock was ancient but solid, but the back door lock was flimsy and had been supplemented with a new-looking deadbolt. A *very* new-looking deadbolt. The basement door was bolted shut with hardware that also looked new.

BJ felt uneasy. She felt worse after she went to make up Cindy's bed. Under Cindy's pillow she found a fully loaded forty-five automatic handgun.

That wasn't like her sister at all.

CHAPTER TWO

Mister Edward West Makes An Appearance

BJ awakened at six a.m. the next morning. The house was freezing cold. She got a fire going in the grate and went to take a walk on the beach while the house warmed up. The weather was sunny, but brisk. Few people were up this hour of the morning. When she set out on her hike, she saw only one person besides herself.

The beach made her feel gloomy. She wanted to be taking her stroll with Cindy. Waves of anger and loneliness washed over her, subsiding a bit, only to come crashing back. She kept taking deep breaths to fight back tears. About an hour later she noticed she was really very cold and a long way from home. She needed to find a place to get a cup of coffee and warm up. She hiked off the beach back to the main road through town and looked around for an early opening coffee shop of some kind. Nothing seemed a likely prospect except for the Embarcadero at the end of the pier. That was a bit pricey for her, but chances were that they were open at this hour.

The hotel and restaurant were built on a pier jutting over a bay where it met the ocean. The view—and prices—were rare. BJ found that she was in luck, the coffee shop opened at seven, ten minutes earlier. Checking her pockets for cash, she ordered a full breakfast to go with her coffee. Being the first—and only—person in the restaurant at that hour, she got a window table right over the water. As she ate, she noticed two men inspecting something in the water near one of the pilings close to where the restaurant perched. She watched them absentmindedly as they seemed to fish about for something floating in the water. When she was about halfway through her breakfast, she noticed a police officer had joined them. He waded out into the water to get a closer look at something. Within fifteen minutes, a crowd had gathered along with a half dozen police officers and sheriffs crowded around the pier. When an ambulance pulled up, BJ could tell they were pulling someone out of the water. Another drowning accident, she thought. She hoped it wasn't a kid and was eventually relieved to see it wasn't. Even from the distance she could tell it was an adult male.

She paid her tab, buttoned her jacket up tightly, and went outside to take a look. Police kept the crowd back, so there was nothing to see but the ambulance pulling away. She resolved to check the local news and see what that was all about.

When she got back to the house, she found the electricity was on, but she still had no heat, and the landline had not been restored. Curious about the gun, BJ went through Cindy's checkbook to see if she could find a payment for it. She found her sister had made an entry for a sporting goods shop and thought that item might be a possibility. If Cindy bought the gun and new locks at the same time, that meant something had made her nervous.

BJ decided she would also go by the antique store while she was in town. She sat down to list out the items purchased for the store that didn't look as if they'd been paid for. In Cindy's ledger she found the following items:

1. Solid cherry wood tea cart $275.00
2. Mother-of -pearl opera glasses $75
3. Ukrainian egg $5.00
4. Crystal decanter set (Waterford?) $65.
5. Secretary $400
6. Chinese box $37.50
7. Spode tea service $135.
6. Malachite table $750
9. Weathervane, horse $17.95
10. Silver candlesticks $20
11. Ship's sextant $15
12. Eagle coin $35
13. Dessert dish $23.50

Exactly thirteen items. BJ wondered if that was an omen.

Adding up what Cindy had paid for them, she found that quite a tidy sum was owed by the store. Enough to keep BJ going for a while. Cindy, being a neat, orderly person, had noted in her ledger not only the date the store reimbursed her, but the check number as well. If the store was going to claim they paid Cindy in cash, it wasn't going to fly. Her trip to the store was delayed while a man from the gas company got her furnace pilot on. While thinking about the utilities, she tried the phone again. It still was not working. Right after the gas man left, there was a soft knock on the door. BJ, somewhat wary, opened it and found a short, stout, elderly woman, bundled up in a coat and muffler, standing on her doorstep.

"Hello. You must be BJ," the woman said in a deliberate voice. "I'm terribly sorry if I'm bothering you. I'm Sallie Wald, the local librarian. I do hope I'm not bothering you. If this is bad time, I can come back. I did try to call first, but I'm afraid I couldn't get through. I don't need much of your time. I just need to collect some books."

"Come on in."

"I'm so sorry about your sister. I feel so callous about my errand. But you see, I'm afraid the library here is quite tiny and the budget is such a problem. I'm afraid I'm not explaining myself well. Your sister, Miss Williams, was one of our better customers, so to speak, a well-read woman and always so pleasant. Came in regularly, she did.

"What can I do for you?"

"I realize this must seem awfully petty to you, but as I said, our library is limited, and we can't afford new books. Not many. You see, Miss Williams checked out a number and we haven't gotten them back yet. I hate to bother you about it, and there's no hurry, but if you would be so kind. When you can get around to it, if you find the books could you get them back to us? I've made a list. I was hoping that would make it easier for you. Of course, I understand that you have so many things to take care of, and there's no hurry, but if you would be so kind, we would appreciate getting them back."

"Of course. No problem."

"Thank you so much. Here's the list I've made up. They're expensive books, you see. Of course, Miss Williams was welcome to borrow them. But some are extremely hard to get hold of, and some we could not replace."

The woman handed BJ the list. No wonder she wanted them back, BJ thought, looking at a list of nearly a dozen books, all listed as hardbacks. She glanced through the list, recognized several of Cindy's favorite fiction authors, and noted three books on Russian history, culture, and antiques.

"Cindy must have developed an interest in Russia recently."

"Yes, yes, so she did. I noticed that myself. She must have been up talking to Mrs. Rybakov who is such an interesting character."

"Who is Mrs. Rybakov?"

"She was a nice old lady who lived on a farm out past town," Sallie said bobbing slightly as she explained. "Spoke with an accent. Told everyone she was from Russia. She's dead now, poor dear. She died, let me see, last April, I think. I've intruded on you enough. If you can get those back to me, we'd be so grateful."

"Oh, no problem. I'll probably have them over to you today," BJ said, hoping her visitor would leave so she could get back to her agenda.

"There's no hurry. Thank you so much for helping us out," Sallie said, bobbing again.

"How did you know I was here, by the way? I just moved in."

Sallie smiled. "It's a small town. People know when you wash out your socks."

BJ escorted her out, shutting the door and turning the new lock.

She frowned. Cindy had become interested in Russian antiques. The Russian lady, Ms. Rybakov, died in April, and Cindy died in May. Could there be a link? And did a Ukrainian egg have anything to do with it?

BJ walked into town and headed down to Antique Row. She stopped at Bingham's first, the place where Cindy had worked. The shop was huge, the size of a warehouse, with three floors open to the public. The first floor had dining sets, oak tables that would seat twenty, sideboards, china cabinets, bookshelves, sofas, loveseats, wingback chairs, coffee tables and end tables. Another section had office equipment, roll-top desks—only two as nice as the one Cindy had, both priced over twenty-five hundred dollars—file cabinets, hutches, computer tables (a concession to the age of technology) more bookcases, desk chairs, and wine tables. The back section was devoted to sofas and living room sets.

The second floor was bedroom sets, dozens of false facades creating the appearance of a room with phony windows dressed with curtains and ruffles, beds, valances, wardrobes, all set to match wallpaper and comforters.

The third floor held all the bric-a-brac with cabinets of old guns, swords, medals, jewelry, silverware, pots and pans from the last century, odd jade ornaments, pictures in heavy carved frames of grim people in faded dress, old bookstands, odd comer pieces, farm implements and livestock tack. This was by far the most interesting part of the store. BJ had thought she could come in and find the items on her list, but that was clearly impossible from the size of the place. It could take her hours to find all the tea carts in the store and she might locate a dozen and have no way of knowing which was hers. She'd have to ask the management about the items. That was not something she wanted to do right now. She wanted to know more about the owners first.

After strolling around Bingham's for an hour, she quit the store to check out the rest of the places. Pine Street had six bone fide antique stores, according to what Cindy had written, though the others sold touristy junk. One of them was a fraction of Bingham's size and sold Oriental items almost exclusively. BJ browsed around for about fifteen minutes, noting the items were all quite pricey. She looked through another showroom, not as capacious as Bingham's, but selling mostly furniture, then checked out a modest glassware shop, a medium-sized about-everything store, and lastly, the place BJ guessed to be Mitch's.

A man she assumed to be Mitch was busy talking enthusiastically to a middle-aged couple about a drop-leaf maple table. Mitch looked to be about forty-five, his hair mostly gray, neatly styled with a braided rat-tail in back. He was tall, slender, and quietly dressed in what BJ guessed were expensive casual clothes. He did seem a bit swishy in his affect while talking to his customers. BJ strolled around the store, noting the quality of the merchandise. Mitch did have some nice things, spendy but not as overpriced as the Oriental junk she'd looked at earlier. She was examining another roll-top desk when Mitch walked up behind her.

"Very nice piece that, but not as nice as the one your sister had. BJ isn't it?"

She looked up sharply. "How'd you know that?"

"Cindy has shown me pictures of you. I'm terribly sorry about Cindy. She was a dear friend. Is there some way I can help you?"

BJ studied him closely. He seemed to have lost all his energy and affect. His voice sounded quietly sad. She shrugged. "I don't know If you can help me or not. I came down to, you know, look at things."

Mitch nodded sympathetically. "If there's anything I can do, you let me know." He gave her a wan smile and headed to the front of the store. She browsed a while longer, then went down to the Riverside Café for lunch.

BJ took a seat at the counter. She still felt nervous to sit with her back to the door, but it was the best way to have a conversation with Kate.

"I tried to call you earlier," Kate said, "but the line was out of order."

"The phone company said I should have service by now. I'll call them again." BJ thought the service should have been restored hours earlier. Everything else was on, and down here, lots of people still used landlines because cell phone connections were so spotty.

"How's the house?" Kate poured her a cup of coffee.

"Cold. Gas man came this morning though. Should be warming up. Say, did Cindy ever talk to you about Russian antiques, or some Russian lady who lived out on a farm, died last April?"

"You must mean old Natasha Rybakov."

"Yeah, that's the name."

"She was quite a character. She'd lived here for better than fifty years. All the locals knew her."

"Was she a special friend of Cindy's or anything?"

"Not special friends. Cindy went up to check out some antiques that Mrs. Rybakov had. She wanted Cindy to tell her how valuable they were. She claimed she had some things from the Tzar's family; that she used to be a maid to one of the Tzar's relatives. Her stories got better as she got older. Last time she told it, she was actually present when Nicholas was executed. She had a lot of nice old things. Most of what she had that was valuable were things she bought in this country. Or that's what Cindy told me. She had some exceptionally fine Ukrainian lace, but Cindy said that most of the things from Russia were junk."

"What happened to her things after she died?"

"Put up for sale. I think everything was sold. She didn't have any relatives. We all thought she'd owned the old house she lived in, but it was a rental, and I hear she hadn't paid rent in years, so when she died, the owner, who was from Seattle, came down and sold everything for a song so he could get the unpaid rent without spending a lot of time here. Cindy bought some things and I got some of the lace. The library got the collection of old photographs and letters. Mitch got the best of the expensive furniture, a sleigh bed, with matching dressers, wardrobe, and vanity."

"How well do you know Mitch?"

"Pretty well, I guess. I like him and Dennis a lot. Cindy liked them both, too. Dennis is black, you know."

BJ nodded.

"Have you talked to the sheriff?"

BJ made a wry face. "Sorta talked to him. He didn't have much to say to me."

"Didn't think he would. Vicky recently reminded me of something though. One of the city police officers is a friend of hers. She might be able to get some information that way."

"Who is Vicky?"

"She's a local writer. She and Mary run The Lavender Nest, which is a bed and breakfast place, and she writes color pieces for newspapers and magazines. I've got her number at home. Why don't I call you later and put you in touch?"

"Thanks. That'd be great." BJ finished lunch and headed back into town. She stopped at the newspaper office and got a copy of the back issue with the obituary for Natasha Rybakov. BJ made a copy, and once back in the Bug, used her cell to try the phone company to see how they were coming with her landline. They informed her the service was reconnected. If it wasn't working, the problem was with the phone or the line. The customer service rep was adamant that nothing was wrong with the service now.

BJ didn't like that.

Once back at the house, she checked the phones and their wall jacks. All seemed to be in order. She went outside to check the line and found the problem. The line was cut where it connected to the house, though it wasn't noticeable without close inspection.

New locks, a new gun, and a cut phone line. BJ didn't like what that was adding up to.

She was cleaning up the kitchen after dinner when Kate came by.

"I tried to call you, but the line's still disconnected so I thought I'd drop in."

"The line isn't disconnected." BJ said. "It's been cut."

"What do you mean it's been cut?" Kate asked, surprised.

"Someone cut the line outside."

"That means he was here," Kate, said, looking shaken. "The person who killed her must have been here."

"It would seem," BJ answered grimly.

"I thought she was killed down near the beach."

"That's where they found her body. If Carstairs knows where she was killed, he hasn't told the press."

"It might have been here."

BJ said, "Might have been."

"Why drag her body all the way to the beach? That seems pretty risky to me."

"I assume the killer didn't want anyone to know where she'd been killed."

"What if he comes back and finds that you're here?" Kate asked.

"Then I'll know who did lt."

"You're not afraid of staying here all by yourself?"

"If I run into the man who killed my sister, he's going to have a lot more to worry about than I am."

Kate nodded sympathetically.

"As long as you're here, would you like a drink?"

"Yeah, I guess so."

"Come on in by the fire."

Kate settled herself into one of the plush wingback chairs near the fireplace, and BJ poured them each a glass of brandy.

"Is that the evening paper you've got with you?" BJ asked.

"Yeah. Want to take a look?" She handed it over. The drowning had made front page news.

> Mister Edward West, staying at the Embarcadero, was found drowned. The police believe he took a walk on the pier in the evening and must have fallen into the ocean. His name was determined initially through identification in his wallet, found on his body. The hotel confirmed he had been a guest there for one previous night and had listed his home address as Seattle.

"Are you looking for anything in particular?" Kate asked.

"The drowning. I watched them fish a body out of the water this morning at breakfast. That name rings a bell for some reason. Edward West . . . Oh, yeah. Cindy's got a letter from him in a desk drawer. Something about buying a sea chest for him."

"Really? Rather odd that he turns up dead."

"Yeah, it is."

"Vicky's police friend might know something about this that's not in the papers. I brought Vicky's phone number. If you get in touch with her, she can get you in touch with the police officer."

"Thanks. I'll try that tomorrow."

"Do you have a cell phone?" Kate asked.

"Yes. Picked one up first thing when I got out. We should add each other to contacts."

"I'll give you Vicky's, too."

After that was accomplished, BJ said, "By the way, the sheriff knows I'm an ex-con, and the local librarian not only visited me this morning but knew who I was, so I'm guessing word is getting around. You may not want to be seen with me. I might ruin what I'm sure is a pristine reputation, failure to salute superior officers aside."

"I can't say that I've led an entirely blameless life. I joined the army because I'd been expelled from Catholic school."

"What'd you do to get yourself expelled from school?"

"I'd gotten hold of some fireworks I was saving for the Fourth of July and hid them in the chapel. One unusually hot day in June, the light from the stained-glass windows set them off and we had two hundred nuns running in panic from the chapel."

"How'd they find out the stuff was yours?"

"Susanne Smith told on me. That's why I got expelled. When I found out she'd snitched, I dumped her down the laundry chute."

"You know, you and I may have more in common than I thought."

BJ went for an early morning walk on the beach, then called Vicky. The woman seemed delighted to hear that Cindy's sister was in town.

"I've heard so much about you," the woman said enthusiastically. "Why don't you come on over to my place later this afternoon? I'll give you directions."

At two-fifteen that afternoon, fifteen minutes late due to having to backtrack when lost, BJ arrived at the snug bungalow on Pirates' Head where Vicky lived.

"I'm so glad you found me. Everyone gets lost the first few times they try. The roads here are so confusing and nothing is marked. They turn this way and that and you have to guess if you're still on the right road."

Vicky Conroy turned out to be a petite middle-aged woman, with curly brown hair, bright brown eyes and a rather birdlike manner of chirping pleasantly when she talked. BJ loved the little house. Constructed of half-timbered pine with huge ceiling beams low ceiling, hardwood floors, huge fireplace, and seemed in every way a beach cottage. The furnishings were simple, but everywhere were piles of books and a blanket near every chair where you could cuddle up and stay warm while you read. The entire south wall was covered with bookcases filled with books. Past the living room was a morning room with windows on three sides looking over the river where it met the ocean. Here was an enormous desk with a computer on it, coffee mugs scattered on every handy place to put one down, and more piles of books.

"Would you like some coffee?" Vicky asked.

"Please."

"Go ahead and have a seat somewhere. I'll just be a minute." Vicky headed off to the kitchen, and BJ took a comfortable seat looking out over the river after removing a pile of books from it. Here, the river met the ocean, and about half a mile off the beach were three huge rocks, hence the area's name, Three Rocks Beach. The beautiful view of river and ocean was framed by windswept pines. BJ had a vague recollection of Cindy telling her something about a pirate ship wrecked on the rocks.

"I was so sorry about Cindy," Vicky brought in a tray of coffee mugs, cream, and sugar. "She was such a well-educated woman. We used to chat about writing and books and movies. She seemed bright without being terribly intellectual. I mean, she read good books, but not books that are good for you, if you know what I mean. The sheriff's office doesn't seem to be getting anywhere. They had one suspect, but it turns out he was in jail when this happened. I don't know if Carstairs has got any more leads or not. He hasn't said anything about it to Lisa recently. You'll like Lisa. She's been a cop for about fifteen years now, but she's still normal, if you know what I mean. She has a very dry sense of humor."

"Did you see a lot of Cindy?" BJ asked, sipping a freshly ground gourmet brew and marveling at how chatty Vicky was.

"After we got to be friends, I probably saw her three times a week. I would drop by her shop and say hello when I was in town. They have lovely things. I would go in and spend an hour browsing. And then she would come out here for coffee, or we'd have dinner together at the Riverside, and we met with Mitch a lot."

"Cindy see a lot of Kate?"

"When she could. Kate stays awfully busy with the café. And she had a friend who used to come down from Portland a lot, though not so often anymore. We used to go there for coffee late at night so Kate could have a cup with us right after she closed."

"Cindy have any other good friends in town?"

"She had a lot of other people in her life. I don't know how close she was to them. Mitch was probably her closest friend. She knew other people socially, but lots of them were her ex-husband's contacts. And of course, because she was black, some people couldn't seem to remember her name. They called her 'that nice black girl at the shop'."

"Did you know she'd bought a handgun?"

"Really? Whyever would she do that?"

"I was hoping you could tell me."

"I couldn't tell you a thing. I haven't a clue."

"I found one in her house and checked with the sports store this morning about a seven-hundred-dollar check she wrote to them, and they told me it matched her gun."

"How odd. No one around here has guns. The men all have hunting rifles, but not handguns."

"Did you know that she'd had new locks put on her doors?"

"No. When was that?"

"I don't know, but they look new. Do most people around here keep things pretty well locked up?"

"Nobody locks anything. The summer houses get locked up for the winter, but the year-round residents never lock up. Probably foolish of us. This isn't the Norman Rockwell town it was in the fifties, but nobody wants to change our country habits. A lot of people don't even lock up at night. The burglars go for the empty rental houses, not ours. Looks like Lisa's car just turned into the driveway. I'll get another coffee cup."

BJ was initially apprehensive about meeting a police officer. She'd had some positive experiences with policewomen until she'd shot a cop. Then her two years in jail and five in prison conditioned her to be wary around anyone in uniform.

Lisa Carter was tan, broad-shouldered, and had thick wavy black hair. She was handsome, and the dimples in her cheeks gave her a warm smile. She wasn't in uniform, but dressed casually in slacks and a flannel shirt. BJ's initial impression was favorable. Her warm smile and firm handshake made it hard not to like her. Vicky made the introductions and settled them all with more coffee.

"I'm surprised you weren't here earlier," Lisa said.

"Believe me, I wanted to be. I wasn't even able to go to the memorial service." BJ said, not wanting to explain that she'd been in prison for killing a cop. She didn't think that would go over too well.

"Are you part of the investigation of Cindy's murder?" BJ asked.

Lisa shook her head. "The sheriff's office shared information with us, but the police department isn't doing the investigation."

"Then you're not involved?"

"Not directly. The sheriff's office gave us the information they had initially so we could match it up with any similar crimes. Any suspects or related information we come across would be passed on to them. They haven't contacted my office about it for months. I don't know if they're still following up any more leads. As far as I know, they didn't have a lot of leads to begin with. She hadn't been robbed. She was wearing expensive jewelry. And she hadn't been raped. No sign of drug use or unusual toxicology results. There are no suspects and there are no theories, as far as we know."

BJ frowned. "You don't have any ideas?"

"She might have been a witness to a crime. It might be a revenge killing from someone in her past. It might be a spurned suitor or stalker. It might have been an aborted robbery. She didn't have any life insurance, so it wasn't for an inheritance."

"If so, I'd be your suspect," BJ said, "since she left me her estate."

Lisa didn't reply.

"And now you've got another homicide to keep you busy." BJ said, sipping her coffee.

Lisa raised her eyebrows quizzically. "I wasn't aware the paper reported the death as a homicide."

"I'm referring to Edward West."

"The man who fell off the pier and drowned?" Vicky asked, joining the conversation.

BJ said, "He didn't fall off after going for an evening stroll last night."

"What makes you say that?" Lisa asked, her voice taking a sharp edge.

"I saw them pull him out of the water. He wasn't even wearing a dinner jacket, only a shirt and tie. Nobody in their right mind would go out for a walk this time of year without a coat."

"Confidentially," Lisa said, "the manner of death is still under investigation. Of course, if he committed suicide, he might have jumped off the pier without a jacket. But that wouldn't explain the time of death problem."

"What's the problem with the time of death?" Vicky asked.

"He ate dinner in the hotel restaurant last night so we know when he had dinner. The analysis of his stomach contents indicates that he died at about two-thirty a.m. roughly. But, if he fell off the pier at two in the morning, the tide would have pulled the body out to sea. In order for the incoming tide to have pushed his body up against the pier, he could not have gone into the water any earlier than four a.m."

Vicky said, "Which raises the question, where was his body for two hours?"

"Say, explain something to me," BJ said. "Why is it that the sheriff has jurisdiction over Cindy's murder, but the police have jurisdiction over the West death?"

"Generally, anything near the beach is county, not city, so the sheriff's office is investigating the death of your sister since she was found closer to the beach line than the city limit line. But this morning, the deputy on duty was rear-ended on his way over to respond. Big problem. One of the first rules of law enforcement is don't get into an accident on a way to a call." She grinned. "Not only was he in an accident, but the cruiser wasn't drivable. So the city police got to the scene first. Otherwise, the sheriff would have had jurisdiction. In that area, we have concurrent jurisdiction since it's right downtown, so it's whoever gets there first."

"There's no doubt that he died from drowning?" Vicky asked. "He wasn't poisoned first?"

Lisa shook her head. "No, the coroner confirms that he died from drowning. Both his lungs were full of water. No marks of trauma on the body. A blood test revealed a high BAC but no other drugs."

"What was his BAC?" BJ had a hunch Lisa knew a lot more than she was telling them and revealing only what was going to make the papers soon anyway.

"Point-two-zero." Lisa answered.

BJ whistled. "I'd be surprised if he could stand up. I don't see how he could have gone out for a walk."

"What's BAC?" Vicky asked.

"Blood alcohol content," Lisa explained. "You're legally drunk if your BAC is point-zero-eight. Point-two-zero is extremely drunk. Anyone but a hardcore alcoholic would be nearly passed out with that high a number."

BJ asked, "Did the medical examiner tell you what his liver was like?"

"His kidneys and liver were normal. He was not a late-stage alcoholic."

"Did he have a lot of drinks with his dinner?"

"According to the hotel records, he had two martinis."

"When was that?"

"About nine o'clock."

"A late dinner," BJ said. "He must have been drinking pretty heavily after that to have a BAC of point-two on a full stomach by two-thirty a.m. Did he have stuff in his room?"

Lisa nodded. "He had his own supply. One of those traveling salesman portable bar kits with gin and vermouth."

"One glass or two?"

"We found only one glass."

"So," BJ mused, "someone else was in the room drinking with him."

Vicky said, "I'm not following your logic. Why does one glass mean two people?"

"Those traveling kits are designed for salesmen, who will normally use them with potential clients. They always come with at least two glasses. If you were drinking with someone and didn't want anyone to know, you would take your glass and hide it or take it away. If he were drinking alone, his glass would be in the room along with a second clean glass."

"How did you learn to think like a cop?" Lisa asked.

"I don't think like a cop. I think like a criminal. Comes from the company I've been keeping over the last seven years," BJ said, getting too close to her history. "So, you think it might have been someone from Cindy's past?"

"I haven't any evidence of that. It's a possibility in any homicide. Was there someone in her past?"

BJ considered the question carefully. "I suppose Bill is a possibility."

"That's her ex-husband, isn't it? I understand that he was the petitioner in the divorce case."

"Yeah, but that was an ego thing. Cindy agreed to that. She was the one who divorced him."

"Why?"

"Because he was drinking and gambling and screwing around too much. She left him and he filed for divorce."

"Lot of hard feelings?" Lisa probed.

"Some. She used to get angry with him, but I think that was over with by the time she left."

"How'd he feel about it?"

"She told me he was pretty pissed off at first. After she moved out, he smashed a lot of the furniture when he was drunk. He seemed to get over it, though. They settled their case, you know. It didn't even go to court. He's remarried."

"He's not holding a grudge?"

"Not that Cindy ever mentioned. There's a letter in her desk about him not paying a credit card debt from their marriage that he was supposed to cover. But I don't think that's revenge—it's only Bill being cheap."

"What'd you think of him?"

"He was good looking, charismatic, ambitious, had a nice family. He was very solicitous of her when they first started dating. Personally, I thought he was an asshole."

"How long had they been married before their problems arose?"

"About an hour and a half. You know how that goes. Guy seems great while he's dating and gets all dictatorial as soon as he has a marriage license."

"Yeah," Vicky said, "that happens often enough."

"What happened to her first husband, John Towerson?" Lisa asked. "I understand that he had the marriage annulled."

This woman has done her homework, BJ thought. "John was a strict Catholic and totally anal-retentive. He wanted the marriage annulled when he discovered Cindy wasn't a virgin."

Lisa said, "I would have thought if those things were so important to him, he wouldn't have married her in the first place."

"I don't think that was the reason," BJ said, "only the excuse. I think the real reason was that Cindy wasn't grateful enough. John expected eternal gratitude from her because he'd been so liberal as to marry a Black woman, and Cindy thought marrying him was doing him a favor. A lot of white men want to have sex with black women, but not marry them. Cindy used to get hit on all the time. She finally started telling guys, 'Hey, if all you want is sex, you got two options, you got your right hand, you got your left hand.'"

"Was Towerson the type to hold a grudge?" Lisa asked.

"Exactly the type."

"What does he look like?" Vicky asked.

BJ pulled out her wallet. Among her photos of Cindy was one of Cindy's first wedding which included Towerson. She handed it to Vicky. "Look like anyone you've seen around town?"

"Not that I've noticed, but that doesn't mean anything. He's pretty ordinary looking." Vicky passed the photo to Lisa, who scrutinized it, shook her head, and handed it back to BJ

"Okay," Vicky said, "so you're drinking with Mister West and you don't want anyone to know, so you slip the second glass into your pocket. Then what happens?"

BJ explained her theory. "You wait until Mister West is drunk enough to be incapacitated and you drown him in the bathtub or the toilet. He's dead at two, but you wait until four to make sure the coast is clear before you heave him off the pier to make it look like an accident."

Vicky said, "That assumes someone who didn't think about the tide."

"If so, there's got to be a way to prove it."

"I know," Vicky said, her voice excited, "find out what kind of water he had in his lungs. If he was drowned in his room, it will be fresh water, not saltwater."

Lisa smiled. "Forensics is probably checking on that now. Sometimes lab results take a while."

BJ put down her empty coffee mug, thinking. "How well do the two law enforcement agencies cooperate?"

"Fairly well right now, despite some general rivalry. Funding depends on successful investigations. Of course, that can cause problems. About five years ago, when Steven Walker was chief of police, he and Carstairs refused to cooperate and as a result, it took them over a year to track down a serial rapist where if they'd pooled their knowledge after the second rape, they'd have known who he was before he raped five more women. That episode is one reason why Walker is no longer chief of police. Carstairs has friends on the City Council and managed to get Walker fired, not for allowing a rapist to be at large for so long as much as for making the sheriff's office look bad."

BJ asked, "If West is a homicide and not an accidental drowning, whose case is it?"

"Probably will be mine. Of course, I will discuss it with Carstairs. If it's related to your sister's death, obviously we should pool our information."

"But won't he end up taking over the case?" Vicky asked.

"No. And Carstairs, for all that he's a macho shithead, is a good cop. He won't keep information from me if I'm working with him. Chances are, he'll tell me everything he knows about your sister's death if we can show a link."

BJ said, "I'll send you a copy of that letter Cindy got from West. It doesn't say much, but it's a starting point."

Later on, BJ thought about Lisa's suggestion that the killer might have been someone from Cindy's past. BJ considered John and Bill as possible suspects. John impressed her as exactly the type to nurse a grudge for years. A second divorce might have been what convinced him that Cindy's "sins" warranted death. But this was a small town. She couldn't see how John could be in the vicinity without Cindy having noticed. As far as she knew, Cindy hadn't had any contact with John since the annulment. She doubted that John had bothered to keep track of Cindy after all these years. There had to be thousands of Cindy Williams listed with DMV and on the Net. Tracking her would have been hard for any amateur to do.

Bill was a different type of man from John: extrovert where John was introvert, but like John, jealous and possessive. She could envision Bill strangling Cindy in a fit of rage if he'd found her in bed with someone else. She had a hard time picturing him doing anything premeditated. But it was possible. Yes, either of them were possible.

On her way through town, BJ stopped at the post office to pick up mail. This morning, she had gone through her sister's letters again and noticed that several, including all those from her ex-husband were addressed to a post office box rather than the street address. BJ knew that Cindy got mail at the house, so she probably used a post office box when she didn't care to have the person know where she lived. Apparently, she didn't want her ex-husband, among other people, to know.

BJ showed the woman at the counter her executor documents to get Cindy's mail, which had been kept in the back.

"We didn't want to return it," the clerk explained. "We knew someone would eventually get around to taking care of it. If we'd known who the estate's attorney was, we'd have sent it there. But since we didn't, we just kept it here and figured someone would show up to claim it sooner or later.

"Thanks for that. I appreciate it"

"Small town here. We're more patient than the big city."

"I suppose some fees are owed?"

"True. You can take care of that now. Or later." The clerk gave her a sad smile. "We all liked Cindy. I'm real sorry about your loss."

BJ took the sack of mail home to sort through it. The phone company had left a note on the door informing her that the outside line had now been fixed. They saved both ends of the cut wires and neatly bundled them up for her. It occurred to BJ that perhaps she had better inform Carstairs about the phone lines.

Once inside, she was pleased to find the phone in working order and called Kate at the café. Kate didn't pick up, so BJ left a message on voicemail, pleased that she now had a working landline and a cell phone as well.

She got herself a glass of wine and settled down to sort the mail. She divided it into four piles; obviously junk, probably junk, possibly interesting and probably interesting. She had sorted through about half, when she found a letter that was in a new category: definitely interesting. The letter was written by Cindy, returned for insufficient address, and addressed to Mister Edward West. BJ opened the envelope and read:

Dear Mr. West,

Thank you for your letter of March 13. I believe I have been able to locate the sea chest you were interested in. It seems it was inadvertently routed to the shop as general ware without the notation of special order. From there, it was purchased by Mr. Eugene Copher, the proprietor of Chang's Dynasty restaurant in Portland. I have communicated with Mr. Copher about the matter and am waiting to hear back. I assume that since he made the purchase for atmosphere in his restaurant, I will be able to find him a suitable replacement for the chest, and he will allow you to take possession. If Mr. Copher is unwilling to return the chest, as is his right, I'm afraid the best we can do is refund your money.

I'm sorry for the inconvenience this has caused you. Please be assured that we are investigating the circumstances that allowed this mishap to occur so that we can take remedial steps in the future to prevent like occurrences.

Thank you again for your patience and continued patronization of our business.

Yours truly,
Cindy Williams

It would seem, BJ thought, that Mister West bought a sea chest through Bingham antiques that had inadvertently been sold to someone else in Portland. She'd better send a copy of this to Lisa. If nothing else, it had an old address for Edward West on it. That might prove interesting.

CHAPTER THREE

A Sea Chest

First Avenue Antiques in Portland was open by appointment only. BJ stood on the sidewalk and gazed through the window. The window displayed a French dining room set, ornate and delicate. Not to her taste. That was all she could see. She pulled out her cell and called the number on the "By Appointment Only" sign. Her call reached a recorded message indicating the owner would be available to answer calls at one-thirty. She was an hour early. BJ decided to stroll through the light drizzle, get some lunch, and try again later.

This was her first trip to Portland in over seven years. She'd always liked the city. She liked being lost in it. She felt, for the first time in ages, as if eyes were no longer on her. No one was staring. In jail, and later in prison, she was watched all the time. At the coast everyone noticed strangers, and some residents blatantly stared at her. She felt as if she lived under constant public scrutiny. Not here. No one paid any attention to her. Being in Portland made her feel *almost* carefree. Not quite.

She was looking for the Chinese sea chest that should have been sold to Edward West. She had found the restaurant owner who purchased it. Eugene Copher was sympathetic and helpful on the phone. He said he was browsing through the antique store looking for items for his restaurant's atmosphere when he saw it being unpacked. The chest hadn't actually been out on the floor. He talked to Cindy, who was in charge that day, and she sold it to him. He paid five hundred dollars for it. He thought she contacted him a week or two later and explained that the chest was a special order and she needed it back. He had obligingly given it back. Cindy made a trip up and put it in the back of her car and wrote him a personal check for the five hundred dollars. He was certain Cindy gave him a personal check, not a store check. He remembered that she'd been pleasant and made a note to himself to come by her store again the next time he was at the coast.

The only other thing Copher was able to tell BJ was that he'd seen a similar chest at First Avenue Antiques, and if she wanted to see what the one he'd bought looked like, she could go look at theirs. He'd only seen it in the window, but it appeared nearly identical.

While waiting for First Avenue Antiques to open, BJ had a hamburger at the Bijou Café on Third. She browsed in the SunBow Gallery until one-thirty and placed the call again. She was able to arrange an appointment for three that afternoon. To kill time, she wandered into a bookstore, bought a cup of espresso, and thumbed through books on antiques and Russian art. One of Portland's greatest assets, she thought, was its combination of book stores with espresso bars.

Promptly at three, she was back at First Avenue Antiques. The proprietor was a haughty middle-aged man in expensive, but-slightly odd clothes. She knew he pegged her at once as not a buying customer and was not the least bit gracious. He did, however, agree to let her see the hand-carved camphor chest. He gave her its origins, age, dimensions, and price, which she noted in a small notebook.

BJ was shocked at the price. "Seventy-five hundred bucks?" she asked.

"And it's a steal at that. If you can find one with a lower price, buy it. Is that all you needed?"

"Yes, that's all I needed. Oh, one last question. How rare are these chests?"

"Not terribly. This is the fourth one I've handled. I know of six that have been sold in other stores in the state in the last twenty years. They're difficult to come by, but hardly one-of-a-kind items."

"Thanks again." BJ flipped her notebook shut, stuffed it into her jean pocket and took her leave. Could this have something to do with Cindy's murder, she wondered, walking back to her car. Why would Cindy sell a chest worth thousands for five hundred dollars? And how much did Mister West know about all this? Funny thing that no one could ask him now. She got back to her car at three-thirty and decided to have dinner in town and head back to the coast afterwards.

She hadn't had dinner in Portland in a long time. Money was no longer a problem. Cindy's lawyer sent her a check for the money Cindy had in savings, which came to a substantial amount. Enough that BJ wouldn't have to worry about paying for dinner. That still gave her a lot of time to kill. She didn't want to eat before six. She wasn't too keen on walking the streets where it was raining again.

She got in her car and headed for the east side of town. She knew where she was going, wasn't too sure why, but knew she was going there. Fifteen minutes from downtown, the Sellwood residential area was one of Portland's most attractive neighborhoods. The river was a ten-minute walk away from most homes. Sellwood boasted several parks along the river, marinas, restaurants and shops, an entire row of antique stores eight blocks long down Thirteenth Avenue. Many homes were turn-of-the-century and beautifully kept up.

BJ parked her car in front of the house she had once rented, a two-story Queen Anne with an old hoary oak shading one side. When she'd lived there, the house was bright yellow with green trim. Now it was white with blue trim. BJ wondered how many coats of paint they'd needed to apply to cover up the neon yellow.

She got out of her car, walked up, and stood ten feet away from the front porch, oblivious to the rain. The door was new. Somehow that surprised her. Of course, they would replace the door in seven years. Even so, she expected to see it the way she had last, with the yellow police tape around it and the door displaying two huge holes. Shotguns leave awfully big holes.

"Willfully, maliciously aimed at his vital organs," the prosecutor had declared.

Aimed my ass, BJ thought. I shot him through the fucking door for Christ's sake.

No trace of that night remained now. The door was new. The house was painted over. The police tape removed and the blood washed off the porch. Not even a trace of a stain. A pool of it had surrounded his body, running off the porch in rivulets and down the stairs. Still, he'd kept bleeding. The pictures of the ambulance gurney showed bloodstains soaked the sheets and mattress and dripped through. He was pronounced Dead On Arrival. He hadn't been dead on the porch. He'd still been alive when they took him. He'd looked up at her with those brown eyes, looking, oddly, like a lost dog.

She'd glanced down at him once, seeing the gaping holes in his chest, the bone poking through. He was heaving with his labored breathing, scraps of flesh flecking his jacket, thrown open wide as he lay on the ground. In her shock, she still noticed the peculiarly rectangular bulge in his side, finding out later that a piece of the door was driven into his chest and out his side.

She looked back in his eyes, and they stared at each other in a mute mutual apology until the EMTs took him away. She remembered stepping back on the porch as they loaded his body on the gurney. Suddenly she started shaking, shaking so violently she thought she was having convulsions. Her body temperature must have dropped because she shivered with cold.

They told her later she had thrown up. She didn't remember that. The uniformed officer kindly gave her his jacket to put on before handcuffing her. Then the police took her away.

She shivered again. February was no time to be standing in the rain. She got back into her car and headed downtown. She turned the heater up to the highest setting to dry her clothes. She hated being cold. The cold was her most vivid memory of her first night in jail. She had to wear sandals with no socks—people hanged themselves with socks—and shivered all night long.

Time to get a drink and some dinner. She went to Oldtown in the hopes of finding Hobo's still open. Still open it was. One of the better, and more expensive restaurants in the area and its clientele was mostly gay. Some lesbians patronized it, but it catered more to men. BJ knew she could hang out at the bar and not worry about being approached. She got a glass of the house Red Classic wine and sipped it slowly. The host had informed her that a table would be available in about fifteen minutes.

She stared at the bottles behind the bar and thought about the shooting. If I had it to do again, would I? What would things be like if I hadn't shot him that night? Probably still looking over my shoulder. Having to stop outside the door at work every night and look over the parking lot to see if he was crouched there, waiting. Having to go over to my house every night to make sure all windows and doors were securely locked, having my heart leap in my throat every time the car ignition coughed, thinking, oh my God, he's wired the car, it's a bomb. How long had I lived like that? Two years? She remembered every time she picked up the paper and saw headlines "woman murdered," she thought, oh, my God, he's found Susan.

Susan was out of the situation, at least. She was safe, somewhere. BJ had heard through the grapevine that she'd made it out of the country to England, or maybe Australia. Out loud she said, "Maybe someday I'll find her. At least I know she's safe."

Would she do it again? You can never take back a killing. Never pay it off, never make restitution. Would she have wanted her life to go on without having had to look at those dying brown eyes? Without having spent two years in jail, three weeks in an inquisition that passed as a trial, five more years in prison, spending the rest of her life, her entire life, with the word "convict" branded on her? If she had it to do again, what would she do? Wait until he got in and aim for his legs? Run out the back? Wait and hope he didn't break in before the police got there? What would she do if she had to do it today?

She took another sip of her wine, pondering the question. "I'd shoot him.

"Madam, your table is ready."

The meal at Hobo's was excellent. She had chicken breasts with marsala sauce and baked potatoes with a shrimp and cheese sauce. After several cups of their house coffee, she was ready to hit the road for the coast again.

Driving along the highway, she thought about the chest. Maybe it meant nothing at all. On the other hand, odd that Mister West would end up dead before a mix-up over a sea chest sold for a fraction of its real value could be cleared up. No, the chest had to mean something. The next question was, where is it now? The guy at the restaurant said he'd seen Cindy load it into her car. It could still be in the car. BJ had no idea what happened to Cindy's car which wasn't at the house. The chest itself was not at the house. She was fairly confident that she would have noticed it if it were there unless Cindy stored it in the basement. Or she might have brought it back to the store. She might have delivered it to Edward West. If it were still in Cindy's possession, or West's possession, BJ should be able to find that out. If it went back to the store, they might have sold it. Of course, if that were the case, they might have a record of the sale. The first thing to do when she got home, would be to check the house and make sure it wasn't still there. Then she had to find the car. She could check with Lisa to see if it'd been reported stolen, or if the police had impounded it. She could also check with Lisa to see if the chest was in the possession of Mister West. Lastly, she could check with the store. She could also talk to Mitch about it. He was supposed to know about Oriental antiques.

She got back to the house around nine that evening. She always felt somewhat depressed coming into an empty, cold, dark, house. As soon as she got inside, she turned on lots of lights, turned the heat up and got a fire going. Only after that did she settle into one of the wingback chairs to read the paper she'd picked up off the porch. She knew she could get her news off the internet these days, but she liked getting news the old-fashioned way and was happy Ocean City had an active press.

Mister West had made headlines again. "Drowning Proved to be Homicide" read the headlines. The city police had declared the death of Edward West to be murder, according to the article. Their decision was based on the difference between the time he died and the time he ended up in the ocean and confirmed by the fact that the water in his lungs was not salt water. The article declared the police to be following several leads.

Well, well, BJ thought, the plot thickens.

CHAPTER FOUR

New Family Members

Saturday brought a stream of visitors to the door. The first was a family giving away puppies. They showed up in a station wagon with the pups in the back, seemingly going door to door to find homes. Small town life. BJ took one. She got a splendid three-month-old female husky-shepherd mix. The dog had a shepherd's black coloring, the broad, confident face of a Malamute, and wolf markings on her head and eyes. A thoroughly fine animal—with enormous paws—and BJ was glad not to be alone in the house anymore. The animal came with a complimentary bag of dog food and a chew-bone. BJ immediately set out papers in the kitchen and got down some bowls for food and water. Her new friend padded happily after her.

The next person to drop by was Sallie from the library. Happy for some company, BJ invited Sallie in for a cup of coffee. She'd brought an additional list of books checked out to Cindy. BJ had already stacked up most of the ones from the first list. She exchanged the stack for the new list and noticed it included a book on Oriental antiques.

Sipping coffee out of a heavy mug, Sallie asked, "Were you and your sister close?"

"Yeah, considering circumstances," BJ said, evasively. "It's been hard for us to see of each other in the last couple years, but I heard from her pretty regularly."

"She tell you about her work?" Sallie asked.

"Yeah, she talked about that and the people she worked with and a little about the locals."

"Did she tell you about old Mrs. Rybakov?"

"No, that's not someone she mentioned, why?"

"No reason. It's just that she was one of our more colorful local characters. From Russia, she claimed, could tell quite a story. I always thought her tales would have made a good book."

"Are you an aspiring writer?" BJ asked.

"No. I love to read, but I don't write books."

Their conversation was interrupted by the puppy, who decided to plant her large and soggy wet paws on Sallie's lap, startling both women into laughter.

"What's her name?" Sallie asked.

"Haven't decided yet. I've only had her a couple of hours. Are you a local?"

"Yes. Grew up here. Went to school back East to get my degree, then came back."

"Didn't want to see more of the world?"

"I'll travel someday. Didn't have time after college. My father needed looking after." She set aside her coffee mug and rose. "I mustn't take up more of your time. Thank you for the coffee and for returning these books."

BJ got to her feet as well. "I'll hunt up the rest."

"Thank you so much. It's not urgent, but we would like them back."

After showing Sallie out, BJ finished her search of the basement and attic for the chest—which turned up nothing—and then hunted through the bookshelves for more library books. *C is for Corpse* she found by Cindy's bed. *Mothers on Trial* she found on the bureau in the bedroom. *West with the Night* was, strangely enough, in the kitchen. *Oriental Gifts, Treasures of the Ukraine,* and *American Antique Treasury* she found in Cindy's library.

She sat down to thumb through the three antique books with her new friend curled up beside her. The first book contained pictures of several chests like the one she'd seen at First Avenue Antiques. Such chests were a common commodity for antique dealers. To BJ's untrained eye, they all looked similar. She wondered if perhaps the West chest—as she had come to think of it—was unique in some way; terribly old perhaps, or one made by a master craftsman, or belonging to some important person. What she read about them seemed to wash out that idea. The chests were built mostly for seamen, captains, and mates. They were only produced in the last few centuries and were not the type of item a master craftsman would create. That made it unlikely that there was anything fantastic about the West chest.

BJ put that book aside and took up *Treasures of the Ukraine*. Most of the book was devoted to history and culture but one chapter on crafts was informative. Ukrainian ware was discussed at length, and with several paragraphs and some pictures of Ukrainian Easter Eggs. According to this book, the shell was emptied of the egg when the egg was blown out a tiny hole at the top. The egg was then painted with geometric patterns. In the pictures, they looked impressive. Lastly, BJ browsed through the *American Antique Treasury*. Cindy may have checked this out for general information. On the other hand, she might have something specific she was interested in. BJ got out her list of items that Cindy had purchased for the store and compared it with items in the book. The book had a long section on tea carts, dessert dishes, and malachite tables.

Her third visitor for the day arrived right after BJ and her new friend finished lunch. Knocking at her door this time was Lisa Carter. The puppy had decided she'd been here long enough to become territorial. She barked. BJ let Lisa in, and at the sight of the tall woman the puppy skidded across the floor in terror. It made both women laugh.

"New addition to the household?" Lisa asked.

"A family came by with a litter this morning. I couldn't resist."

"What's her name?"

"Doesn't have one yet."

"So you're calling her JD for Jane Doe for the time being?"

"That's an idea."

"Then when she eats your favorite slippers you can call her JD for juvenile delinquent. Then when she's old enough to lay down the law on her priorities it can be short for 'jurisprudential doctorate'."

"Hey JD, what do you think about that? JD sound okay to you?" BJ asked. The puppy peered from around the corner, wagging her tail. "She seems okay with JD. Come on in and have a seat." They settled themselves in the library where BJ found a comfortable chair.

Lisa said, "You know we've determined that Edward West was murdered."

"Saw it in the paper."

"We found your sister's name and post office box in his address book. Any idea why?"

"Because of an antique Chinese sea chest. I'll get you the letters." BJ showed the letters to Lisa as well as the pictures of the chest in the book. She explained her trip to Portland and what she had found out.

Lisa said, "I can't see what this has to do with either death, but it may be a connection. Finding the chest could help."

"I've spent all morning checking the house. I've gone over every inch and the basement, attic, and garage, and it's not here."

"Then it could have gone back to the shop, or to West."

"Or it could still be in her car. That's what I wanted to ask you about. What happened to Cindy's car?" BJ asked.

"I don't have any idea. Might have been impounded. If so, the sheriff would know about it. Don't you have a legal document releasing her things to you?"

"Yeah. From the probate lawyer. That's how I got into the house."

"Why don't you run down to the Sheriff's office on Monday and check into it? He won't be there today or tomorrow and I'm not available until Tuesday afternoon."

BJ grimaced. "The sheriff isn't exactly my favorite person. And I doubt that I'm his, but I'll check it out. If he has the car, do you want me to leave it there for your people to check out?"

"That would be best."

"I don't suppose you're going to tell me how your investigation is going."

"Too early to say anything. We're interviewing everyone, the hotel staff, the dining room people, anybody in the vicinity. We'll get a search warrant to check his home, as soon as we find out where it is, check his criminal history, and talk to everyone listed in his address book. We can't really form theories until we've assembled available data. 'Always a mistake to theorize without data'," Lisa quoted from the Sherlock Holmes book, *A Study in Scarlet*.

BJ nodded. "I'll let you know if I find the car."

"Thanks. I'll be in touch."

BJ saw Lisa out and sat down again to think. If Cindy had written a personal check for the chest, then when she gave it to West, he would write her a check. If she had delivered it, her bank account should show a five-hundred-dollar deposit. BJ went to the desk and looked through the records. She found the right month, but no such deposit was listed on the bank statement. That made it unlikely that Cindy delivered the chest to her customer. She'd know more on Monday.

She thought about Lisa's statement that the cops would search West's home when they found it. Since he was identified from the ID in his wallet, he probably had a driver's license with an address, but the letter Cindy sent him had come back in the mail which seemed to indicate West moved months ago and hadn't updated his address like your average normal, law-abiding citizen would do. That seemed curious.

Another visitor arrived after four. Vicky dropped by on her way back from town. JD barked furiously at them both for thirty seconds and then hid in the kitchen again.

"I guess you've found out by now that West was murdered." Vicky said, taking a chair in the library.

"Yes, Lisa was by earlier."

"I don't suppose she gave you any inside information."

"No. Took an official line, 'inquiries are being made, too early to say.' I gave *her* information." BJ went on to explain about the chest and letters.

"I wonder if that's enough to do murder for," Vicky mused. "You wouldn't think so. From what you say, that chest can't be worth more than around five thousand dollars if you believe the dealer saying his was a steal at seventy-five hundred. More likely it's only worth five-K, and he's charging a dealer mark-up at seventy-five hundred. That wouldn't be enough for me to do murder."

BJ said, "I've done a little checking in some books, and it's doubtful the chest was so unusual that it'd be worth more."

"How odd that Cindy would sell a chest worth thousands of dollars for only five hundred dollars. She must've known what things are worth. I can see her buying something for less than its value, but not selling under the value."

"My feelings exactly. I'm sure Cindy knew what she was doing when she priced things."

"Now you're going to find the car and the chest as your next step?"

BJ said, "That's the plan."

"Lisa will give us general info, but she won't tell us anything confidential, not about a pending investigation. We'll have to do our own detective work."

"We?"

"I know something about digging up information. I used to be a reporter. I'll bet I can find out a few things. I'm sorry this involved your sister. I really liked her."

"So did I."

Vicky looked over at the pile of books on the coffee table. "Doing some research?"

"Oh, those belong to the library. Sallie was by earlier and gave me a list of books Cindy had checked out."

"Poor Sallie. How devoted of her. She probably does that on her own time."

"Why 'poor' Sallie?"

"I feel sorry for her. She's well educated but came back here after college to look after her father who was an invalid. She looked after him full-time so she couldn't hold down anything but a part-time job so she survived on that and his social security. He left a pile of debts when he died. She spent years paying them all off. Of course, the library position doesn't pay her much, even though she's full time now, so she's always lived just above the poverty line. It must be trying to live in a rundown apartment, buy all your clothes used, get a five-hundred-dollar car every few years, have your vacation consist of not going to work with nothing to look forward to but a retirement on Social Security."

"Doesn't sound like much of a life. She never married?"

"No. I doubt if her father would have let her, and by the time he died, she was well in her thirties and I suppose she always thought of herself as too old."

"Were Cindy and Sallie on friendly terms?"

"Quite friendly terms, as far as I know. They're both well-read women and Cindy used the library a lot. Do you mind if I look around the house a bit? I haven't been here in a long time."

"Be my guest. Oh, wait a sec, speaking of detective work, take a look at this list." BJ handed her the list of thirteen items.

"What is this? A scavenger hunt?"

"These are items Cindy bought at sales that the store may or may not have reimbursed her for. If so, I need to find out. Let me know if you spot something on the list in the house. I've determined that nothing in the house could possibly be a tea cart, but I don't know about dessert dishes, or some of this other stuff."

"I probably won't be of any help. Antiques aren't my line but I'll try."

They went over the house together and found what might be the dessert dish and the mother-of-pearl opera glasses. Vicky said, "I don't know if that's the dessert dish she was referring to, but it might be. You can tell it's old. But those are definitely mother-of-pearl opera glasses."

"Since she put them away in the house, I think we can reasonably guess that the store does not owe her any money for them. But that can't be true of everything on the list. The teacart and the malachite table are definitely not here. That must mean she had them delivered to the store. Have you talked to them?" Vicky asked.

"Not yet. I don't know them at all. If I have to haggle with them over this stuff, I want to know something about it first."

"You ought to show this list to Mitch. He'll help you out."

"Yes. I was going to go by sometime this week and ask him about the chest, too."

"One last thing before I leave. I was wondering if Mary and I could drop by tomorrow and get some comfrey plants. Cindy has a lot in the backyard. We transplanted some last spring but the elk ate them."

"Yes, I saw that elk were a problem here. There's an elk crossing sign by the golf course. What happens when you're golfing and you run into some?"

"You let them play through."

BJ laughed.

"Can we get some comfrey from your yard?"

Still chuckling, BJ said, "Fine by me. What is comfrey?"

"An herb. You make tea with it, and it's a natural antibiotic."

"You want to get that now?"

"No. Cindy has foxglove in back, too, and I don't trust myself to tell the difference. Mary knows them well. She can tell them apart, but I can't until they get their blooms. Their leaves look very much alike."

"What is foxglove?"

"A plant with lovely purple flowers, but it's poisonous. The leaves contain digitalis. About three years ago an elderly couple mistook foxglove for comfrey and made tea with it. They both ended up in the hospital with heart attacks and one of them died. The man had a weak heart to begin with. Anyway, I don't want to get them mixed up."

"You're welcome to come back and get all the comfrey you want. JD and I may be at the beach, so go on back and help yourself."

"Thanks. I'll see you tomorrow."

BJ and JD were at home when Mary and Vicky dropped by the next day. They had gotten back from a walk on the beach. JD approved of the beach wholeheartedly. She came home happy but exhausted and promptly passed out on the couch.

BJ got out of her wet clothes and showered and changed. She had just put on a pot of coffee when Mary and Vicky came by. Doctor—"Mary to her friends"—Stout proved to be a roly-poly woman in her fifties with a bright smile and laughing eyes. She was a retired professor of English Literature and her main hobbies these days was herbalism and birding, Vicky introduced them and BJ started thinking of them as "the laughing sisters" since they seemed to do that a lot. She took them out back to the yard, once nicely landscaped, but now sadly neglected and dreary looking in the February rain. Mary pointed out the comfrey and foxglove plants. The comfrey was all near the garage, while the foxglove was alongside the house. Mary gave them a mini-lecture on the two plants growing on the property when Cindy bought it. Mary also pointed out the sage, basil, rosemary and mint, in the now overgrown herb garden. They retired to the house, discussed the West case, and the West chest, and then Mary and Vicky took their leave.

BJ drove into town to do her grocery shopping. JD came with her, delighted to ride in the car, and happily preoccupied with a marrow bone as BJ went into the store. BJ was glad of the company. Her dog,

Nikki, was placed with relatives when BJ was arrested. Nikki, a three-year-old golden retriever, was now happily ensconced in a family with five children. They had kept in touch to the point that the family sent her a picture once a year of Nikki and the kids. BJ had also had two cats, but she had no idea what had happened to them. Probably simply adopted new owners, she thought. Cats did that. She probably ought to get another one. A house was not a home, in her opinion, without a dog in the yard and cat in the window.

She thought about it and decided she may as well be prepared. She bought cat and dog food when she did her grocery shopping. By the time she had gotten back to the car, she'd made another decision, something else to add to list of things to do on Monday: get a cat.

Once home, she put the laundry away and started preparations for dinner. BJ was a fair cook. She'd learned a lot of cooking while living with Susan. Susan cooked not at all, so BJ learned fast with some help from Lee Lynch's *Butch Cook Book*. She'd experimented with the basics, developed a few special dishes, and could do something passably gourmet in a pinch. She ought to get Kate to teach her how to make that wonderful black molasses bread. Kate knew a thing or two about cooking.

Cooking was now a special activity, since she could do it for herself and have whatever she liked. She had hated prison food. The only way to make it palatable was to work out on the exercise machines to the point that you didn't care what you ate as long as you could eat something.

Prison had offered BJ little to do. She tried taking some of the classes, but most were too elementary for her. She read whatever she could get her hands on. The prison library was limited and consisted mostly of donated romances. Being able to get a book she wanted from the outside was always a challenge and a delight. Even so, she couldn't read all day. She worked while she was there. She did housekeeping, worked in the kitchen briefly, worked in the welding shop for a while, and finally settled in as a trustee in the health department. The work was menial but she got to hang around with doctors, nurses, and a physical therapist who all helped satisfy her curiosity about medical treatments.

BJ also exercised whenever possible. Weightlifting gave her something to do and alleviated the stress. As a result, between bad food, no snacks and lots of exercise, she was now lean and muscular. She was going to have to start jogging to stay in shape, she thought, as she prepared her shrimp gumbo.

She was curled up with a book in the study when Kate dropped by. BJ had an open bottle of wine, and quickly filled two glasses with a nice Pinot Noir.

"Thought I'd see how you're doing," Kate dropped down in a chair by the fire. "Who's your new friend?"

"This is JD. I got her yesterday." BJ noticed that Kate was dressed in casual clothes, jeans and a flannel shirt, so she hadn't come from work. BJ thought the clothes not only flattered Kate, showing off a trim figure, but their casualness made Kate look at home in BJ's chair, which she liked very much.

"She's beautiful." Kate said, petting JD.

"Yes, she is," BJ said, not thinking about the dog, "but she needs a cat."

"The house needs a cat. This would be a good house for a cat. It's warm."

"That's what I hated about prison, always cold."

"You were involved in the Patrick Hunter case, weren't you?" Kate asked, still stroking the dog. Kate looked at her directly, but with the firelight flicking over her face, BJ couldn't easily make out her expression. She didn't see accusation or revulsion, but neither did she see sympathy.

BJ raised her eyebrows. "Involved in it? I *was* the Patrick Hunter case."

"What happened to his wife?"

"She went underground and got out of the country."

"Have you heard from her?"

"No."

"I remember reading about the case in the paper."

"So I heard. Dead cops get good coverage."

"You didn't read the papers?"

"I was in jail."

"Does it bother you to talk about it?"

BJ shrugged. "Sometimes. In stir, all anyone wanted to talk to me about was what happened. I got tired of everyone asking. Don't take it personally."

"Sounded to me like self-defense. From what I read."

"It was self-defense. Jury didn't think so. They didn't like the fact I shot him through the door instead of shooting him in a face-to-face confrontation."

"Why did you shoot him through a door?"

BJ sighed. "I called the police as soon as he showed up. This had happened before. It had happened a *lot* before. The one time he got into the house he managed to nearly kill Susan before I got him off her. He still had time to break my arm before the cops showed up. Susan was in the hospital with a fractured larynx, three broken ribs, a sprained neck and two black eyes. I had a broken arm. He claimed that Susan invited him over to pick up some of his things. Not true. She didn't have any of his things at my house. He said while he was there, we got into an argument. He claimed we were at the top the stairs and I lunged at him, but Susan grabbed me and pulled me back, and then I backed into her and we both fell down the stairs. He claimed he hadn't hit either of us. That didn't exactly explain the smashed chair, which is what he broke my arm with."

"That sounds ugly."

"So, anyway, Susan didn't think she could handle a jury trial, so that case was tried before a judge. He didn't believe me or Susan, said something about illicit relations being provocative, but he didn't exactly believe Patrick either, so Patrick was convicted of violating a restraining order and misdemeanor assault and put on bench probation. That means he didn't have a probation officer, he's on probation to the judge who won't know what he's doing unless he gets arrested again, and sometimes not even then. He was put on paid administrative leave by the police while they supposedly investigated the matter. I don't know what they did by way of investigation. Susan and I both gave statements to the IAD. Patrick gave them his version of events. They refused to look at Susan's medical records, didn't think those were relevant."

"Doesn't sound like their hearts were in it."

"They took his gun away from him during administrative leave, but he had a collection, so that didn't change anything. Susan and I started getting threats and for various reasons thought that was coming from other cops."

"Didn't he have to do any jail, time, pay a fine, anything else?" Kate asked, looking incredulous.

"Judge gave him a three-hundred and seventy-five-dollar fine that he never paid. He was supposed to get counseling but he never did. The judge said the sentence was light because he had no other criminal convictions, but he'd been found guilty of violating the restraining order four times before this. After everything that happened, some judge told him to pay a hundred dollar fine, which he never did, and to leave Susan alone, which he didn't do either. He came back to the house about six months after his conviction. I don't know what set him off that last time, and he was usually violent after he'd been drinking all night. It wasn't late—only about eight o'clock—but he was roaring drunk. He pounded on the door, then kicked it. I called the cops. I got the shotgun and worried this time he'd brought his gun. We couldn't actually see him from a window because he was too close to the door. We yelled at him to stop. Susan told him the cops were coming, and I told him I had a gun. He knew I had a shotgun. I told him that when he was in court the last time, that I had a shotgun and that I'd use it if he ever showed up again. I figured that the second he got in through the door, he'd start firing. He was kicking it right where the lock was, and the door jamb was cracking, ready to break, so I fired. I fired twice with a twelve-gauge loaded with double-ought buckshot. And that's all she wrote."

BJ got up and put another log on the fire. "How about you? What do you do for excitement?"

Kate gave her a sad look. "I'm sorry I upset you."

BJ shrugged.

"I mean it, BJ. I'm very sorry all that happened to you. Thanks for trusting me enough to explain it to me."

BJ let out a sigh and sat back down again, secretly relieved that Kate seemed to understand. "Let's talk about something else. How are things at the restaurant?"

"Good. Business is slow this time of year, but it's not bad. We get in enough locals to stay busy."

"Hey, play scavenger hunt with me." BJ handed Kate the list of missing antiques. "Know anything about these? Cindy bought them and I don't know if she gave them to the store and still needs to be reimbursed or what. We found the mother-of-pearl opera glasses and we think we found the dessert dish. Everything else is still fair game."

"Let's see. I remember that beautiful malachite table that was part of the Rybakov estate. Cindy bought it for the store, a pretty valuable piece. As I recall, the store was going to reimburse her after they sold it because they had a prospective buyer, and Cindy was going to get a commission."

"You know what it looks like?"

"Yes. I was with her when she bought it."

"Do you know if it's still at the store?"

"I don't know. Tell you what, I'll drop by the store on my afternoon break and look. Want to come with me?"

"I have to go down to Westport tomorrow and talk to Sheriff Carstairs. Believe me, I'd rather spend the afternoon with you. Anything else on the list ring a bell?"

"The Spode does. She got that for Lynn. I'm sure of it. Lynn is a friend of hers in Portland who also has an interest in an antique store as well as an interior design business. Lynn collects Spode. I remember that she mentioned the Chinese box being quite valuable or terribly over-priced and she wasn't sure which. Mitch might know about that. The Ukrainian egg she got for herself as a kind of a reminder of old Mrs. Rybakov. Gaudy looking thing, gold paint and studded with rhinestones and green glass. The ship's sextant she mentioned too, but I forgot what she said about it. Make me a copy of the list and maybe it will come back to me."

BJ copied out the list and handed it to her.

"What are you seeing Sheriff Carstairs about?" Kate asked.

"Cindy's car. No one seems to know where it is. Lisa Carter thinks it may have been impounded after the murder and kept by the sheriff. I'm going to check that out tomorrow."

"Speaking of cars, did you know that one of your tires is going flat?"

"Yeah, I noticed. I guess I'll have to take it in to a Les Schwab tire place before I drive to Westport."

"Why don't you borrow my car and take your tire in when you're not planning a trip?"

"Are you sure you wouldn't mind?"

"No. I won't be going anywhere. Just walk over to the café tomorrow and pick up mine."

"Great. I'll do that."

"Looking for anything in particular in the car?"

"The West Chest may still be in the car. By the way, how is your friend from Portland?"

BJ couldn't mistake the anger and hurt in Kate's frown. "She was supposed to come visit this weekend, but something came up. Again." Kate rose. "Well. I'd better be off."

"No hurry. I don't have any plans for the evening."

"Thanks, but I have to be at work by four. Pick up the car any time."

"Thanks a lot. See you tomorrow then."

BJ went up to bed shortly after Kate left. JD curled up beside her. She lay awake thinking about Patrick Hunter and her broken arm. One time, Patrick had come over, drunk and belligerent, and pounded on the door before trying the latch and finding it unlocked. Susan and

BJ both raced upstairs, locked the bedroom door, and called the police. The dispatcher said they'd be right there. BJ remembered counting every minute that went by on the bedroom alarm clock. Susan talked to Patrick through the door, trying to calm him down. That worked for almost fifteen minutes. Suddenly Patrick flew into a rage and slammed his shoulder into the thin, interior door. It cracked. He gave the door a hard kick and it broke, swinging inward.

Susan had said calmly, looking him in the eye. "Patrick, you can't go around kicking people's doors in. The police are on their way. If they find you here in violation of the restraining order, they'll arrest you."

"You fucking cunt!" he yelled. His fist struck like lightning, blackening both Susan's eyes and knocking her to the ground. He jumped on her, breaking three of her ribs. His big hands gripped her around the neck and fractured her larynx. BJ grabbed him from behind in a choke hold, pinching the carotid arteries on either side of his neck. He stumbled backwards, somehow managed to gain his feet, and slammed BJ into the wall. Her grip slipped, and he slung her to the floor. She managed to get up on one knee before he swung a chair at her head. On instinct, she raised her left arm to ward off the blow. The chair broke her forearm, but missed her head.

Slightly out of breath, Patrick paused before swinging the chair again. BJ got to her feet, and managed to block the chair with her right arm, smashing what was left of the chair. A well-placed kick caught Patrick in the groin, sending him to the floor.

Susan tried desperately to suck air in through her swelling throat. BJ stood blinking in pain. Her arm felt as if a fire was working its way to her shoulder.

Two minutes later, Patrick recovered and stood up. Shit, thought BJ, here we go again. I should have kicked him when he was down. She had no idea he would recover so quickly. She thought he was down for the count. He was reaching inside his coat for something when the police showed up. She never did find out what but assumed it was a gun.

BJ got a ride to the hospital with a friendly woman cop. The EMTs were able to get a breathing tube down Susan's throat before the swelling larynx blocked off her air passage entirely. Patrick was taken down to the station, booked, and released on a misdemeanor assault charge.

Tonight was the first time in a long time that she'd thought about her broken arm. It had ached off and on for a year, but she had full use of it. Now her arm only ached when cold. Thinking about Patrick and the deaths threats she and Susan had received, BJ got out of bed, retrieved Cindy's gun from the drawer, and put it on the nightstand beside the bed. She knew the doors and windows were locked. After getting her arm broken, she never went to bed without checking.

CHAPTER FIVE

A Prowler

The next morning, BJ debated taking her tire to Les Schwab's to have it fixed, but since Kate had generously offered her car, she decided to deal with the flat some other time. She and JD walked down to the beach for a stroll and then went to the café. Kate gave her the keys to her Subaru, and BJ and JD headed south.

BJ's first stop was the library to return half a dozen books. The county library was an old building, but meticulously kept. Sallie greeted her at the entrance and expressed appreciation for the books being returned.

"Some of these go back to the main state library," Sallie explained. "I had to order them for Cindy since we don't keep them in stock. We have a respectable collection of books on antiques, being right on the coast, but those are of a more general nature."

"Nice old building," BJ said.

"Yes, it is." Sallie took off her glasses and polished them. "It served as the courthouse in the last century when this was the county seat. We took it over nearly fifty years ago. Couldn't get county funds to refurbish it, of course, too expensive. Got a grant from the federal government since it is of historical interest. Since then, we are kept in shape by local artisans who practice their carpentry and masonry skills here. It's a joint enterprise with the community college trades program."

"What's this here?" BJ peered into a room where the walls were decorated with a peculiar collection of guns, knives and odd memorabilia.

"That's the mystery room. Come on in and have a look. You see, we have enough room that the books kept in the regular docketing manner are in the upstairs rooms, and we have these extra rooms on the first floor that we've turned into theme rooms. We have an extensive collection of mysteries, my favorite, and so popular here on the coast. On a stormy night, most everyone likes to curl up by the fire with a good mystery. In addition, we have the treasure room. The books there are devoted to buried treasure, Spanish galleons, shipwrecks on the coast, things like that. It's very popular, too. We have another theme room that deals with Native American culture and crafts. The biggest theme room is for marine biology, though biology is a somewhat inaccurate description. Books on marine life, forest ecology, hiking trails, things like that, are in the biology room."

Sallie took BJ on a quick tour, showing her the other theme rooms. In addition to books, they included pictures, charts, and artifacts dealing with the various topics. BJ appreciated how much more interesting the collections were than endless rows of shelved books. She paused in the treasure room to glance at some of the books. Treasure hunting seemed intriguing and romantic.

"I'll have to stop by again on my way back and browse through," BJ said, putting a book back on the shelf.

"Are you going somewhere?"

"I've got to go down to Westport and talk to the sheriff. Probably take all day. He thinks if he keeps me waiting long enough, I'll leave. After that, I want to get a cat. Say, where is the county pound?"

"Come on in to my office, and I'll draw you a map. The animal shelter is off the beaten path and hard to find if you aren't familiar with the area."

BJ glanced around as Sallie took a seat at the desk to draw her a map. Sallie's office was the most organized room BJ had ever been in. A huge desk at one side took almost the whole length of the wall, each stack of papers tucked neatly into a box, the pen and desk set in order, a calendar in the corner, and a Rolodex and pad near the phone. Two wingback chairs sat in another corner near a table where a coffee set with pot and cups stood at the ready on a lace table drape. A bookshelf covered the entire back wall. Scattered among the books were plants, brass ornaments and gargoyles, but all looking neatly tucked into place. Another bookcase in the rear of the room had locked glass doors, presumably for rare editions. On a wine table next to the bookcase was a pitcher for water, a drinking glass, an extra pair of glasses, and several medicine vials. BJ noticed one was Valerian, the other Digitalis.

"Here you are. I hope this will help." Sallie handed BJ a piece of paper with streets neatly drawn and labeled. "I've penciled the number of the pound in the corner in case you get lost."

"This is great. Thanks. Say, does Valerian work for you? I've heard about it, but never tried it."

"I find it very helpful. But like everything else, if you use it too often, it loses its effectiveness. Also, you have to be careful not to spill any, because cats love the odor, and you'll have every cat in the neighborhood at your doorstep if they smell it. Good luck with Sheriff Carstairs."

"Thanks a lot."

"And do come back when you get a chance. If I'm not here, Judith will be, and she's the expert on the treasure room."

"I should be back around four. Will you be open that late?"

"We're open until five every weekday."

"So, I'll see you then."

Sallie politely walked BJ out to the car and waved goodbye.

BJ took JD out for a walk before going to the sheriff's office. As she had predicted, the sheriff kept her waiting an unnecessarily long time. He did, finally, manage to give her a few minutes of his time. BJ suspected he only did so in order to leave for lunch. She explained her errand. He checked a file and brusquely informed her no vehicle was impounded. No such vehicle had been located, and his notes did not show any registered to Cindy Williams.

That was odd, BJ thought. What the hell happened to Cindy's car? It wasn't found in the vicinity of the murder. It wasn't parked at the house. If it was left on a street somewhere, the police would eventually have been notified. As heir to the estate, BJ now owned the car, and the sheriff had an obligation to provide her with any information about it. Despite how unfriendly the sheriff was, she didn't believe he was lying.

Was this a clue of some sort? Or did someone read about Cindy's murder in the paper and simply steal it, knowing no one would report it missing right away?

After finishing with the sheriff, BJ took JD for another walk on the beach. When they'd reached the point of exhaustion, BJ felt safe to get some lunch without having to worry about JD eating the car. She found a nice restaurant and finished lunch around two, took JD out for another walk, and went off to find the pound.

After half an hour of careful selection and filling out the requisite forms, BJ acquired a rust-colored cat. Sekhmet was barely out of her kittenhood and had selected BJ. As BJ had entered the cat room to look around, Sekhmet reached out a paw and gently tugged on her sleeve until she got BJ's full attention. The event confirmed BJ's belief that humans don't choose their cats; cats choose their humans. After pledging her life and immortal soul that she would have the cat to a vet to be properly seen to in the immediate future, BJ managed to negotiate the use of a pet carrier for the trip home. Once she got the kids settled in the car—JD insisted on another walk—BJ stopped by the library on her way through town. Sallie was not in, but another librarian was happy to discuss the treasure room and recommend some books.

BJ got home just after five. She watched her new family members scout around the house for a while, then drove Kate's car back to the café, dropped the keys off, and walked home.

She noticed something wrong after she finished dinner and went in Cindy's library. First, the book she'd been reading was no longer on the floor by her chair but was now on the table. The coffee mug had also been moved. BJ alertly went over the house, and in every room, she could find some minute detail revealing the recent presence of an intruder. In her absence, someone painstakingly went through the entire house, attic to basement, looking in all the drawers and nooks and crannies.

She thought it must be a pretty bold burglar to make an illegal entrance with her car parked right in front. A careful examination of the doors and windows revealed no signs of forced entry. Whoever got into her house either had a key to one of the doors or had come down the chimney. She found no scratches on the locks to indicate the use of a lockpick. BJ had seen locksmiths work a lock, and knew it left definite signs. That meant her intruder had found a way to steal keys from Cindy—or someone was close enough to Cindy to have been given a key.

Since Cindy's car was missing, someone presumably had Cindy's keys, which would include keys to the house since they would not have been changed after Cindy's death. Why had the intruder come in? Because he had left clues the police overlooked? Or to find something?

She decided she'd better tell Lisa about this tomorrow and get her locks changed.

Before going to bed, she double-checked the doors and windows to make sure they were locked and bolted. The deadbolts were turned from the inside, so there was no external key needed, which gave her a small amount of comfort. She made sure Cindy's gun was loaded and next to the bed. And she felt very grateful that JD was now a member of the household. If the pup heard any sounds in the house, she'd be up and barking. Of course, then JD would cower and hide, but sounding the alarm was all BJ needed.

First thing Tuesday morning, BJ tried to reach Lisa Carter. She was informed that Officer Carter would not be available until later that afternoon. Next, she called Kate and gave her an update. Kate, in turn, had news for her. The green malachite table was still at the store, waiting to be sold. Kate had chatted with the manager about it and discovered the prospective buyer hadn't panned out, but he was trying to get a buyer from Seattle interested. BJ crossed the malachite table off her list of things to find. She tried calling Lynn in Portland, having ascertained from Cindy's address book that Lynn was Lynn Langford of Through the Looking Glass Antiques. Lynn wasn't in, so BJ left a message. Next, she called Mitch and set up a lunch date for the next day.

Having run out of detective work for the moment, she took JD out for a walk, dropped off her tire at Les Schwab's, and called a local locksmith to come change the locks.

The locksmith, Robert "Marty" Martin took one look at BJ and started talking about his recently deceased husband. BJ pegged him as being in his mid-sixties and in good shape. He wore unscuffed work boots, clean and pressed jeans, and a lightweight windbreaker over a T-shirt. Chatty and friendly, he had no reservations about answering any of her questions.

"So, you knew Cindy?"

"Oh yeah, I knew your sister. She's a good friend of Mitch Quigley's, and he's in my church. They're welcoming, you know, praise the Lord."

"These deadbolts here look brand new."

"Yup. She had new ones put on the door about a week before she died, poor thing, and she had me check her window locks and replace all of the worn hardware. Place was tight and secure when I finished, let me tell you, God bless us. No one was going to break into the place."

"Why? Did she mention why she did that?"

"No, she didn't say anything to me about why."

"I've never known my sister to have a firearm. What do you know about that?

"Not much. She didn't say anything to me about a gun. No idea why she wanted extra bolts. Most people down here don't bother— not the year-rounders, at least."

"Someone got in though."

Marty squatted down and picked up one of the deadbolts he'd removed. "Whoever got in here yesterday had a key. I can tell you that much. You can tell when someone's used lockpicks, and in spite of what you read in fiction, not everyone and their mother goes running around with those. You have to get bonded and checked out before you get a locksmith license, let me tell you. But that's not the half of it. Learning to use those things is the real challenge. Jesus, Joseph, and Mary, it takes years to learn how to do it fast, especially on locks like these—they're hard to get through. So that's why I sold 'em to your sister. God rest her soul."

"Anybody come to you lately with a mold or drawing to create a key?"

He put down the deadbolt and rose. "Nope, nobody's asked me to do a key from a mold of any kind. Ya read about that in fiction, some-one making an impression of a key in wax or clay or chewing gum and getting a duplicate. Never in my forty-six years in this job has anyone ever asked me to do anything like that. I'd a been asking a few questions about it, as God's my witness. I don't ever help anybody do anything illegal."

"That's smart," BJ said.

"There, that should do it for you. These here will keep out everybody but the Angels. God bless now."

Later that day, to BJ's relief, she discovered Sekhmet was familiar with the purpose of a litter box and did not require any further instructions regarding its use. Sekhmet had made friends with the dog, after a sort, and found the top of the mantel to be her favorite place to curl up for a nap. She seemed to be adjusting splendidly to the new household.

BJ scheduled an interview with Lisa late that afternoon and headed into town. She let JD out of the car and said, "Sit."

The dog looked at her expectantly but actually sank down on her haunches.

"Good dog," she said in a voice dogs always seemed to respond to. "Good girl. Now stay."

She backed up, and JD whimpered. BJ made a hand motion and repeated "Stay" several times. JD looked like she wanted to bolt, but she obeyed the command. After a moment, BJ went back to her and petted and praised her, rewarding her with a long walk, then left her in her car while she went into the police station

The local station was a compact place, low-ceilinged, and almost claustrophobic. She still felt uncomfortable around people in uniform, particularly when lots of them were congregated in the same place, but she kept her discomfort in check while she talked to the detective.

BJ said, "The sheriff's office never recovered any car belonging to my sister. Unless the sheriff's lying to me, which I rather doubt. He has a legal duty to turn it over to me since I'm the heir."

Lisa frowned. "The car would have been impounded if left at the scene, or her house, or found somewhere else after being reported as abandoned. Are you sure your sister had a car?"

"Yeah. She's got receipts for her insurance at the house. I contacted DMV, and they gave me the details. She had a Volvo V90 wagon. Here's the license plate and VIN." BJ said, handing a piece of paper to Lisa.

"Let me check on this. I'll make sure we don't have a stolen vehicle report."

"Would you know if it was junked?"

"Oh, yeah. Junk dealers report the VIN to DMV every time they junk out a car. Odd that it hasn't turned up. It must mean something."

"By the way, does Sheriff Carstairs come from a wealthy family?"

"No. He's a local boy. His father was a fisherman and his mother was a housewife. They were both locals. Why do you ask?"

"No particular reason. It's just that I don't know too many people who manage a Rolex on a sheriff's salary."

"I wasn't aware that he had one. You sure it's not a knock-off?"

"He was wearing it each time I've seen him, and yeah, I'm sure it's not a knock-off. I worked part-time for a jeweler when I was working on saddles with lots of silver, and I can tell the difference.

Lisa shrugged. "Insurance money from his parents' deaths probably."

"By the way, did you find out anything interesting about Mister West?"

"Real name is Westophal. He's from Seattle and has a curio shop there and in Hawaii. Best of the West, he calls it. He's done some business with the shop where your sister worked, bought things through them now and then. That's all I can tell you.

"Okay, thanks. Please, get back to me about the car, if you find out anything."

"Sure will. And you let me know if you turn up anything."

"I'll do that," BJ promised.

Wednesday BJ had lunch with Mitch. He had suggested the Dory restaurant close to the strip of antique shops at the north end of town. Getting there after the lunch rush, they were able to get a seat by the window where BJ could see Pirate's Head and the trio rocks at Three Rocks Beach. She couldn't help but envision a pirate ship sailing into the rocks. Mitch was dressed in black dress slacks, a white button-down dress shirt and black leather tie. He wore a single gold hoop earring, which also reminded BJ of pirates.

After the coffee arrived and the server took their order, BJ said, "I was wondering if you could help me with something. I'm trying to find out what happened to the items listed here." She handed him the scavenger hunt list. "I think Cindy bought this stuff for herself or the store, and I need to find out what happened to everything."

Mitch studied the list. "The shop has the malachite table. I know Cindy bought a dessert dish for herself. She mentioned that. She bought the Ukrainian egg from Mrs. Rybakov's estate as a memento. I would guess that she bought the Spode for Lynn. I'll bet the 'Oriental box' is the jewelry box I've got in my shop. She got that at an estate sale, and I've been trying to move it for her. We split the profit on these things. I'm fairly sure she sold the tea cart to Velda Cox. She owns that bookstore-coffee shop near the Esplanade on the highway. I'm not sure about anything else. Does this list have anything to do with her death?"

"Not that I know of. I'm just trying to get her estate in order. You wouldn't have any idea what happened to her car, would you?"

"She had a Volvo wagon, didn't she? Haven't the police found it?"

"No. It seems to have disappeared off the face of the earth."

The server, a pretty, young Latina woman, wore a nametag indicating her name was Rosita. She set down bowls of clam chowder. BJ grabbed her spoon and dove right in. Unlike what came from cans, this chowder was chock-full of fresh clams as well as potatoes and bacon pieces large enough to be identified as bacon.

Unlike BJ, Mitch dipped carefully into his soup. "That's odd, isn't it? I always thought that if you left your car too long anywhere, they towed it away eventually. Sure it's not at the junkyard?"

"The police are checking those records to see if its VIN has been recorded in their books, but they checked once and couldn't find it."

"If I were you, I would go talk to Alfred."

"Who is Alfred?"

"He's the junk man down at the junkyard. I don't know if he owns it or what, but the car may have shown up there and not gotten the number recorded in the books. I mean, if the car was in good shape, it may have been sold."

"If so, DMV would have a record of it."

"Not if it were some type of under-the-table sale. Not that you can sell a car under a table, but you know what I mean. Maybe someone skipped the formalities about registering it. Some of the guys at the junkyard may not be all that honest. Anyway, Alfred would know."

"If Alfred were selling cars under the table, so to speak, would he tell me?'

"Absolutely. He's the soul of honesty, our Alfred. A bit slow, but thoroughly honest. Someone may have got the car and not reported it for some reason, thinking Alfred would know to keep his mouth shut. But if Alfred knows, he'll tell you. He might get talked into doing something that wasn't wholly legal, but only if he did not recognize it as illegal. He's gotten in some trouble not following all the regulations for his business, but never because he was intentionally trying to do anything wrong. "

"Do you know anything about an Oriental sea chest Cindy bought for a man named West?"

"That rings a bell. You mean the restaurant chest? The one she sold to a restaurant by mistake?"

"Maybe? What do you know about that?"

"She sold it off the dock. You see, we get deliveries all the time, if business is good, and you put it on display even before it's checked in so it makes your inventory look full. I always call that 'off the dock.' We do sell things that way, occasionally. Something comes in and you have it unpacked and in the dock section of the store waiting to be checked in—you know, put on your inventory list—and a customer wants it the second you've got it unpacked. So she sold this chest off the dock to a man who was opening a restaurant and wanted it for atmosphere. Later she found out it was someone else's special order. She had to go buy it back."

Their waitress appeared with their entrees, razor clams for BJ and fish and chips for Mitch. BJ's entrée came with a fragrant rice pilaf, lemon wedges, and sautéed fresh vegetables.

"Can I get you anything else?" Rosita asked with a bright smile. BJ still found it odd and slightly unnerving to be treated as an ordinary person after so many years of being treated like an unpredictable dangerous animal. She and Mitch both indicated they were fine.

BJ said, "Do you know if she ever delivered it to the man who ordered it?"

"Right before she died, she dropped by the store after we'd closed to chat and mentioned that she was going to Portland the next day to get the chest back, so I don't know what happened. That was the last time I ever saw her. I'm not sure if it was two or three days before her murder. I'm very sorry that happened, you know. I liked your sister so much."

"How come the guy, West, that is, was writing to her at her post office box? Why wasn't he writing to the store?"

"I don't know. I think Cindy generally used her box for business matters."

"But her boss knew about it?"

"Oh yes, oh yes. They both knew. She must have caught Jim on a bad day when she told him. He flipped out and screamed that she was stupid, and you know what? He called her the N-word. In front of my customers and staff! He apologized profusely afterwards, even took her to dinner, but still. That doesn't make up for it, does it? Get someone in a bad mood and they show their true colors. You know what I mean, don't you?"

"I sure do. Have you ever done any business with this guy, West?"

Mitch shook his head. "Never heard of him. Aside from what I've read in the paper." Their server appeared to refill their water and coffee. By now the place was filling up again with retirees and people who had time on their hands and didn't need to use the noon lunch hour. BJ noticed an elderly woman, thin and somewhat haggard, staring at her from several tables away and wondered what that was all about.

"Lisa tells me West is an antique dealer. Got a shop in Seattle and Hawaii."

"Really? And I've never heard of him. How strange. We dealers tend to chum around a bit, you see. Odd that he shops in this part of the world and I've never heard about him. And he has a shop in Hawaii, you say? Well, isn't that peculiar?"

"Isn't what peculiar?"

"Jim ordering a chest from Hawaii for a customer who has a shop in Hawaii. If this West fellow has a shop in Hawaii, why didn't he buy the chest there? Why ship it here?"

She and Mitch finished their meal, took care of the tab and headed off in different directions. BJ went back to the house and found she had a message on her machine from Lynn Langford. She called back but couldn't reach Lynn. She talked to another woman at the shop who said Lynn would be in on Thursday morning and if BJ dropped by the shop, she would be able to talk to Lynn. BJ left a message that she might be by. She thought about driving down to the junkyard to talk to Alfred, but she hadn't yet picked up the repaired tire.

The rest of the afternoon was spent getting the tire back on her car, buying some more groceries, walking the dog, and attending to household chores.

Thursday morning BJ was up bright and early to walk JD. Vicky and Mary had agreed to take JD for the day so BJ could drive up to Portland. She dropped JD off at their house after their walk and headed for the café. Kate, as usual, was busy with her customers, but managed a few minutes of conversation.

While BJ wolfed down steak, eggs, hash-browns, and toasted black bread, she gave Kate an update on what Mitch had told her and about the intruder in the house. Kate mentioned that she'd seen Sheriff Carstairs outside the post office in a long conversation with Steve Kilpper, Cindy's former boss. She assumed it might have something to do with Cindy. Kate couldn't think why else Carstairs would be talking to Kilpper.

BJ thanked her for the information, got a cup of coffee to go and headed up to Portland.

As she drove, BJ figured it unlikely that the shop would be open before ten. The weather was poor, raining again, but BJ was buzzed from the coffee and hot on the trail, so she felt relaxed and at ease. The mild rain made for a pleasant drive, even if she was worried enough to have put Cindy's gun in the glove compartment of the car.

Lynn's shop was in Multnomah Village, a part of Portland, slightly south of Portland proper. The main strip was lined with antique and craft shops, an old-fashioned candy and ice cream store, Fat City Café, three bookstores, and a post office. A great place to spend a Saturday browsing, BJ thought. She found Lynn's shop and strolled in. It had an unmistakable English flavor to it, with innumerable tea sets, tea carts, tea clothes, and old English furniture. She asked for Lynn and was directed by the sales woman to an office where a woman sat at the desk working at a computer.

BJ's first impression of Lynn was favorable. She was an attractive woman with a rather flat broad nose, full mouth, and dark brown eyes. Though her expression was serious, she had good-humor lines at her eyes. BJ put her age at about forty-five. She smiled warmly as BJ introduced herself as Cindy's sister.

"I got your phone messages. Cindy mentioned she had a sister. Good to meet you." Lynn rose and shook BJ's hand. She had a pleasant low, gravelly voice that sounded like stream water running over pebbles.

"Sorry to bother you at work, but I wanted to check something out with you."

"Don't apologize. I'm happy to help in any way I can."

"I've been going through my sister's papers, trying to get everything in order." BJ paused as Lynn nodded knowingly. "And I'm trying to track down a Spode tea service. Mitch said you might know something about it."

"Which one?"

"This one." BJ handed her the cancelled check showing the purpose.

"Oh, yes. Lancaster Rose pattern. That's the one she gave me. To sell, I mean." Lynn reached in her desk and handed BJ an envelope. "As you can see, I've had some trouble delivering the check."

BJ noted the envelope had first been mailed to Cindy's box, then to the attorney who had handled Cindy's divorce, and then returned to Lynn.

"Let me make this out to you, and I'll tear up that other check," Lynn said, drawing another check made payable to BJ McKay.

"Thanks."

"I don't suppose it helps to tell you how fond I was of your sister, but she really was an awfully nice woman. I'm so sorry about what happened."

BJ dug her fingernails into her palms to not cry. She regained her composure and went on. "I'm also looking for these other items on the list. I've made a check mark by the ones I've found so far. You wouldn't know anything about the other items, would you?"

Lynn took the list from her and studied it. She shook her head and handed it back. "I'm afraid I can't help you. Say, you haven't heard from a woman named Velda, have you?"

"No, why?"

"She has a tea shop at the coast and handles some antiques. She handled a few things for Cindy on commission. I have a vague memory of Cindy saying she was going to pick up a tea cart at the DuBoff estate sale and have Velda handle it on consignment. Cindy often did that. She would buy things at garage sales and estate sales and either have Bingham's sell them on consignment or some other shop like Mitch's or Velda's."

"Why would Velda be calling me?"

"I got a very odd phone call from her about two months ago. I was down at the coast and I bought an antique tea pot from her, something else from the DuBoff estate sale. It's about two hundred years old and quite a collectible. I doubt Velda was aware of that. I got it for considerably less than market value. Velda isn't an antique dealer. She runs a tea shop and sells a few things on the side. So anyway, she called me about three weeks later and not only accused me of robbing her—and I can see why she is upset about selling something for less than value—but she went on and on and on and talked about a conspiracy to put her out of business and people being out to get her. Sounded to me as if she had some mental issues, but I don't know if she would have any problems with Cindy over a tea cart placed there on consignment. Oh, that reminds me, I think that the DuBoff's estate sale had an old sextant for sale."

"You wouldn't know anything about an Oriental sea chest Cindy sold to a restaurant owner in Portland and then bought back to sell to the customer who had ordered it, do you?"

"No. What's all that about?"

BJ explained in some detail. Lynn's brow furrowed and her mouth formed into an attractive pout as she digested this information.

"That does sound odd," Lynn agreed. "And this man West is now dead?"

"Murdered."

"Very odd. What was the name of his shop again?"

"Best of the West. Has one in Seattle and one in Hawaii."

"Never heard of it. Never heard of him, either. Let me check something." Lynn pulled out a magazine on antiques and thumbed through the advertisements. "He doesn't advertise with the rest of us. Let me check something else." She got a catalogue of dealers for an antique fair and checked the index on it. "He's not listed here, either. I wonder what kind of business he does."

"I've got the address of his shop in Seattle and his home address. His real name is Westophal, and he's the only one listed in Seattle. I thought I'd hop up there this afternoon and poke around a bit."

"Mind if I come with you? I'm curious about who he is and why I've never heard of him."

"I'd love to have the company. When can you get away?"

"Now, if you're ready."

"Great. Let's go."

Lynn stopped to give some instructions to the saleswoman and get her coat. BJ refueled on coffee and they headed off to Seattle.

"Do you know the men Cindy worked for?" BJ asked as they crossed the Columbia River and headed into Washington.

"Steve Kilpper and Jim Marsh? Yep. I know them. I used to have a shop down at the coast and know everybody in the business. That's how I met Cindy."

"What are they like?"

"Marsh is a bit of a stick, in my book. I still run into him at sales and auctions from time to time. He's always polite but not friendly. He's a good businessman, though. Runs the shop well in that respect. He has no aesthetic sense whatsoever. Cindy was a real help to him in that regard. She had a great instinct for quality. I think they got along okay but strictly a business arrangement. I mean, I don't think Cindy ever mentioned going out and having a cup of coffee with him. She said she liked working for him. He was particular that all the accounts be kept correctly and the paper trail on everything be in order, but he trusted her judgment on a lot of things as long as she dotted all her I's on the paper work. He gave her a lot of free rein on other stuff. They trusted Cindy to buy for them, and I think she's the only one at the store they let do any purchasing.

"Steve Kilpper is about the opposite type of personality. He can be glib and charming one minute, and morose and abusive the next. He's nice looking. I met his wife, once, at an auction. One of those basic, sally-rally stand-by-your-man types. Kilpper must be doing pretty well, judging by the way his wife dresses. She's got some designer stuff, some Cartier jewelry, and used to drive a DeLorean. Now I think she's got a Benz."

"Could that be her own money?"

"No. That woman didn't come from money. You can tell in this business. I've got a fair number of customers who do come from money and believe me, you can tell."

"Who else worked with Cindy at the store?"

"They keep a fair-sized staff of sales people, probably over a dozen. Turnover's pretty high there, too. Probably Kilpper's management style. The woman who does the books is Charlotte Gibson. She's been there nearly ten years now, single mother raising a son, so not the type to be changing jobs too fast. Eddie is probably the most experienced salesman. He's been there since God was a child. Ken Somebody-or-other runs the loading dock. He comes to mind because I know Cindy didn't like him. I can't think of anyone else off the top of my head."

"Was Cindy seeing anybody?"

"A man you mean? I don't think so. She had a couple of dates after her divorce, but what she told me was that she wasn't interested in getting involved with anyone. I don't think she saw any one guy more than twice. Except Mitch. They were good friends, but not romantic, of course."

"Anybody recent?"

"Not that she told me."

BJ lapsed into silence, digesting Lynn's comments. She probably ought to get more information out of Mitch about any possible boyfriend in the picture. She should also talk to some of the other staff members see if any male coworkers imagined a romance and it turned ugly. She had a hunch the bookkeeper, Charlotte, would be the best bet there in terms of gossip.

Lynn picked up the conversation again and they talked about the antique business on the coast versus the city and then about more general topics.

Once they reached Seattle, they used Lynn's phone to track down "Best of The West" since BJ was no longer on speaking terms with her

GPS. The shop was one enormous room with a peculiar eclectic selection of antiques and oddities. BJ wandered around aimlessly, not knowing what she was looking for other than some sort of sea chest. Lynn, on the other hand, was a woman with a purpose. She looked around carefully, repeatedly summoning the sales people to answer questions about merchandise. After nearly an hour, Lynn made a purchase and indicated she was ready to leave.

"What did you think of the place?" Lynn asked as they walked back to the car.

"Kind of an odd collection."

"A *very* odd collection. Either he hasn't been in business long or he won't be."

"Why do you say that?"

"He's doing a lousy job running his shop. In the first place, this is the wrong part of town for it. He's next to a sporting goods shop, a pet store, a car dealer, and a bank. In the antique business, you want your shop in an area with similar shops. Secondly, no theme or focus to that shop. It's not good stuff, it's not junk, it's not a particular period or style. It's not organized in any fashion. None of his salespeople know anything about the merchandise but the price. I can't believe anyone could run a store like that and be successful."

"What did you buy?"

"A turn-of-the-century teaspoon. They charged me fifteen dollars. It's a popular collector's item, and they sell for between two and three hundred dollars. Fifteen dollars is horribly underpriced, but then their end tables and china were all overpriced."

"Maybe the store's a front. Let's go cruise by his residence."

"You have his home address?"

"Yep, found it in Cindy's papers."

"Let's go take a look."

Consulting the GPS several times, they found their way to an obviously affluent neighborhood and located the address. Three things struck BJ about the residence of the late Mister West: that it was expensive, very large, and impressively defended. They could glimpse enough of the home through the bars of a security fence to see bars on the lower windows of the place and notices of video cameras. She and Lynn stared at it for a while before heading back to Portland.

They stopped in Centralia, Washington, another antique hub, for a late lunch at the Olympic Club.

"He's got money coming in from somewhere," Lynn said, as she drank from a pint of Ruby ale.

"You can't always tell by the house which might be mortgaged to the hilt. He may not have had a dime of equity in it. If he was into something like conning people into letting him invest their money, he'd create a front that would include a prosperous-looking business and a prosperous-looking home. That's how Ponzi schemes are usually run." BJ took a bite of her Captain Neon burger thinking that other illegal operations like drugs were also run that way. She had met several grifters and numerous drug runners in prison. She'd learned from them exactly how to flash-cook meth and why you should never do that.

"Lots of fencing and iron-work for a gated community house."

"Don't you think it's kinda odd the store was still running given the fact the man is dead now?"

"I'm guessing the crew working there is used to no supervision. That's the impression they gave me," Lynn said. "I like your idea of a false front to get investments. That would fit."

They finished lunch and continued south. BJ dropped Lynn off at the store in Portland and drove back to the coast.

She arrived at Mary and Vicky's cottage around seven that evening to pick up JD.

"I hope JD wasn't any trouble," BJ said as the puppy greeted her with great enthusiasm.

"No. I gave her some sandals I was planning to throw out and she had a great time." Mary held up some unrecognizable items of leather.

They all laughed.

Mary insisted that she stay for a bowl of homemade soup, fresh bread, and salad.

"Did you find out anything interesting during your trip?" Vicky asked.

"I've settled the matter of the Spode tea service, so that's crossed off my list. We also checked out West's shop and home address in Seattle. According to Lynn, he was running his shop as a rank amateur, but he sure lived high and mighty, judging by his house. He also has a hell of a fence, iron security gate, and barred windows."

"Sounds like he was running drugs," Vicky said. "The store must have been a front."

BJ said, "That's the same evil thought that occurred to me."

"Certainly possible," Mary said. "I wonder if that's what the sea chest was all about. That would explain why he so badly wanted to get that particular chest back. Maybe it's full of drugs or money."

Vicky arched an eyebrow. "And no one knows where it is?"

"I guess not," BJ said.

"Learn anything else from your trip?" Vicky asked.

"Lynn gave me a rundown on some of the people Cindy worked with at the store. I thought I'd hit you folks up for a second opinion. Do you know a woman by the name of Charlotte Gibson?"

Vicky said, "That's the bookkeeper, isn't it? I've met her once, but I don't know anything about her. Any reason you want to talk to her?"

"Couple of reasons. I want to see if any of the other items on my list are at the store. She might know. I also thought it possible that some employee at the store had a grudge against Cindy. You know, scorned advances."

"Cindy never mentioned anything like that," Mary said, "but doesn't mean it didn't happen. You must have read in the papers about cases where an employee decided he was in love with a woman he worked with and killed her even though they never dated."

"Do you know a guy named Ken?" BJ asked. "Lynn said he worked the loading dock."

"Oh, yeah," Vicky said. "I've run into him before. Actually, he ran into me—backed into my car once. His name's Ken Stearns and he's an actively practicing alcoholic. Cindy never had any particular trouble with him that I know of, but generally he's an asshole. I can see him committing a crime, but not getting away with one."

"And who's Eddie?"

Mary said, "That's the other salesman, the one who's been there for a while. He's gay. We run into him now and then. He seems okay. Anal retentive type, though. He and Cindy weren't particularly close."

"What are the partners like?" BJ asked, noticing the soup was excellent.

"Fire and ice," Vicky said. "Jim is moody, up and down, and Steven is uniformly business-like at all times. Cindy never warmed up to Steven, but never had trouble with him either. Jim was alternately a great joker and good company, or a schoolyard bully, jovial but hot-tempered. I think Cindy got along with both of them but didn't like either of them."

"I don't suppose that Lisa Carter has passed on anything interesting to you two?"

"No," Mary said, "but we intend to do some sleuthing of our own. We'll let you know what we come up with."

First thing Friday morning, BJ went to the county courthouse and got two interesting pieces of information: the name of the legal firm that handled the Rybakov estate, and she found out Kenneth Stearns had three restraining orders filed against him, all by different women, none of them Cindy. Since the old Russian lady died without a will, the probate court appointed a lawyer to handle the estate to make sure the county, which was owed lots of back taxes and incurred a variety of other expenses related to the death, got its money. BJ knew it wasn't unusual for a property owner who wasn't paid rent on a regular basis to ignore property taxes if he had a cash flow problem and just let the eventual sale of the property catch them up.

She'd thought about a coworker as a possibility, and here Kenneth Stearns had a history of violence against women. Cindy could have had reason to feel threatened, hence the new locks and new gun, the type of response a person would make if they were being stalked. The most likely stalker would be a predatory man, either a sex offender or someone who considered himself spurned, likely someone who crossed paths with Cindy on a regular basis. A clerk at the post office, a server in a coffee shop, or someone she worked with who had a history of committing abuse, sex crimes, or stalking behaviors. Mister Kenneth Stearns, who worked with Cindy on a daily basis, appeared to have a history of stalking behaviors. She needed to talk to Lisa to see if Lisa had ever considered him a serious suspect and if he'd ever been questioned by the sheriff's office.

BJ knew restraining orders were not the same thing as criminal convictions and were obtained upon one person's sworn statement. That's why the district attorney who prosecuted her didn't consider Patrick Hunter dangerous with only one minor criminal conviction. Never mind all the times Hunter had violated the restraining order. BJ started to get mad all over again just thinking about it and had to put her feelings aside. Again. Right now, what mattered was Cindy. She could have all her feelings later. Perhaps the sheriff looked for convicted felons in the immediate vicinity as potential suspects and had not checked TRO's. She would have to find out.

After leaving the courthouse, she looked up the address of the law firm Escobar and Cooper on her phone, made an appointment for that morning, and, after walking the dog, headed down the coast.

CHAPTER SIX

Lawyers

The firm of Escobar and Cooper boasted six attorneys—four associates and the two partners. Vernon Cooper was the attorney who handled the estate matter. After a five-minute wait in the outer room, BJ was ushered into his private office. Cooper, a spare man in his late sixties, had gray hair, neatly cut, a nicely tailored but casual suit, and a slight shake to his movements. He looked straight from central casting with his cautious thoughtful gestures, somber appearance and intelligent expressions. His office furnishings, like his clothes, were of good quality, but not ostentatious. BJ was sure his clients felt assured of his professionalism.

Once she seated herself in one of the two antique Hepplewhite chairs, he said, "I understand you've expressed an interest in the estate of the late Natasha Rybakov."

"Yes. I understand my sister may have purchased some items from the estate, and I'm trying to track down everything to make sure her estate is in order."

"And your sister is?"

"Cindy Williams. She died nine months ago."

Mister Cooper nodded sympathetically. "Yes, I remember reading about that in the paper very sad occurrence, very sad." He took off his glasses and polished them as he shook his head in a regretful manner. Replacing his glasses, he looked up at her with a thoughtful expression. "And how is it that you think I may be able to help you?"

"She wrote checks for a number of antiques, some for herself and some for her store. I'm trying to track down everything she purchased. Some of the items I've accounted for, but not all of them, and I don't even have enough of a description of some things to be able to recognize them. I understand she wrote a check for a Ukrainian egg she purchased from the estate sale. I can't find it, so I wanted to make sure it was delivered—the egg and some other things. I'm not sure what else she may have bought from the estate. Here's a list of the items I'm looking for." She handed him her scavenger hunt list.

Mister Cooper peered over the list, holding it under his desk lamp. He studied it a moment, then looked back at her. "The Ukrainian egg, I'm fairly sure, was purchased from the estate. I believe the tea cart and weathervane may have also come from the estate. If you will permit me to make a copy of this list, I will have my secretary check it against the estate inventory and be able to confirm that for you."

"That'd be great. Would your records show if the items were delivered or picked up?"

"I can check that information for you and send it along."

"I'd appreciate it. I'm impressed with your memory."

"My memory may be flawed, but a review against the inventory list will be accurate. The Ukrainian egg I remember because our local librarian inquired about the estate donating it to the library as a curio, the egg and some other items of minor value. The tea cart I remember because I'm an Anglophile and do take afternoon tea. I admired the one at the estate auction but handling the legal aspects of the estate, I could not bid on anything. I think Velda Cox may have ended up with it for her Victorian Tea Room on Main Street."

"I certainly appreciate your time," BJ said politely, glad that he would charge his time to the Rybakov estate and not to Cindy's.

"Not at all. I'm happy to be of assistance in any way I can."

Back at the house, she fixed lunch, walked the dog, and headed into town. She found the Victorian Tea Room right off Highway 101. The Tea Room, perched over a brook running through a wooded lot in back, offered a selection of tasteful teas and dainties for a mid-afternoon repast. Tables near the window overlooked the brook with more on another wall where customers could sit and look out over the ocean. BJ noted that in one corner, between the shelves of tables and tea accoutrements was what she presumed was a cherrywood tea cart. BJ took a seat near the window on the brook side and ordered a pot of Assam tea and light cucumber and ham-paste sandwiches. After waiting for a few minutes, she strolled over to the tea cart and examined it. While obviously old, it seemed in good shape.

"Lovely old piece, isn't it?" asked the matronly-looking woman who delivered her order.

"Yes, it is. I've been looking at these at Bingham's and they don't have any as nice as this one. Are you the store owner?"

"My sister and I own it. I'm Theodora Cox. My sister is Velda."

"You get this down here at the coast?"

"At an estate sale. You don't find many old ones like that these days. Adds just the right touch to the atmosphere, doesn't it?"

"Yeah, it's real nice. Buy it from some English people?"

"Russian lady. But the table is English. Solid cherrywood."

"I thought I saw something like this at the antique store here in town."

"Bingham's, you mean. Those are replicas of antiques. This one is genuinely old."

BJ resumed her seat and ate her food. After the meal, she went over to Bingham's and toured the store again, looking for anything that might be on her list. She saw dozens of silver candlestick holders and a number of crystal decanter sets, but no way to tell if the ones on the list were in the shop. They had several weathervanes, but none of a horse, no ship's sextant, no gold coins, and no eggs.

"Can I help you find something?" a salesman asked.

"Actually, I was trying to find Charlotte Gibson. Is she here?"

"Yes, in the back office on the second floor, past the antique desks and buffets."

"Thanks."

Charlotte proved to be an attractive woman in her mid-thirties. When BJ tapped on the open door to the back office, Charlotte looked up, stared a minute, raising her eyebrows.

"You're BJ McKay, aren't you?"

"Yeah. Good guess."

"I remember seeing your picture in the papers."

BJ raised her eyebrows at that.

"Can I do something for you?" Charlotte asked.

"Yeah, actually. I was hoping I could talk to you about my sister."

"Cindy Williams."

"Right."

"I get off work at five. Maybe we could get some coffee or something."

"I live not too far from here. You wanna come over and I could throw something together for dinner?"

"That would be great. My boy is staying with some friends so that will work out real well. Where do you live?"

"You know the house Cindy had?"

"That cute Victorian on Pine Hill?"

"Uh huh."

"I know where it is."

"I'll see you after five."

"Great."

As BJ got up to leave, someone out on the show floor screeched, "You're trying to put me out of business! Well, it won't work. It won't work, you bastard, it won't work,"

Curious, BJ left the office to see what the commotion was about and Charlotte followed. The woman facing BJ was clearly the same one who'd stared at her at the Dory restaurant when she'd had lunch with Mitch. The woman was now was yelling at a man in a suit who BJ assumed was one of the owners.

"You can't do this me," the woman screamed, spittle flying from her lips. "I'll kill you first. You stole my hope, Kilpper, now this—you bastard. But you won't get away with it. I'll kill you first. I'll put a bullet right between your beady little weasel eyes!"

A man dressed in jeans and a flannel shirt grabbed the woman by the arm and roughly dragged her outside, nearly tossing her off the steps.

"What was that all about?" BJ asked.

"Velda is really losing it," Charlotte whispered. "She's *really* losing it. I heard she did something like this to Mitch a couple weeks ago."

"How long has she been acting this way?"

"She came around about a year ago and got mad at Kilpper for selling a hope chest to someone else she'd wanted to buy, but she wasn't this bad then."

"What's a hope chest?"

"Usually a cedar chest. Girls used to keep their blankets and embroidered kitchen cloths and tablecloths in a chest in hopes of using them when they got married, hence the term 'hope' chest. I was always hoping I'd have a chest." She laughed, looking down at her ample bosom. "Velda wanted to buy one we had about a year ago, but Kilpper said it was a special order and wouldn't sell it to her."

"And was it?"

"Maybe. He's never liked Velda. She bad mouths everyone in town when she can. That's been going on for years."

"Did she have a problem with Cindy?"

"Not that I know of."

"Who was the lumberjack who just threw her out?"

"That's Ken. He works here, mostly unloading cargo."

"Ken Stearns?"

"You know him?"

"Heard about him."

"Hey, I gotta get back to work. I'll see you tonight."

On the way home, BJ picked up a nice pinot noir wine, a couple of steaks, and some fresh crab for cocktails. Charlotte arrived promptly at a quarter after five. They chatted amiably about the weather as they put together a tossed green salad and threw the steaks on the grill. They piled the kitchen table with mashed potatoes, crab, salad, fruit, garlic bread, steak, and wine, and sat down to work through the food.

Charlotte said, "So glad you've come to town, BJ. I've been meaning to contact someone for a while, someone who was handling Cindy's affairs. A few things have happened at the store I thought you should know about."

"Oh?"

"You know Cindy used to buy things for the store?"

"Uh huh."

"She'd buy pieces at sales, and if Kilpper liked them, the store would reimburse her, pay a small commission, and sell the items. She bought a bunch of things before she died, and the store never paid her. In fact, Kilpper told me to go ahead and list the invoices as paid. He said he was making a deal with the estate attorney, but I know he never did."

"Do you remember what the items were?"

"Some of it, yeah. A malachite table, a secretary, a decanter set I remember. I made out a list. I have it at home. I knew Kilpper would pull a stunt like this.'"

"Just a sec." BJ rose and went to the desk in the living room. She returned with the scavenger list and handed it to Charlotte. "These are items I'm trying to find. Any idea where some of these might be?"

Charlotte set her fork down and examined the sheet of paper. "The tea cart Cindy sold to Velda Cox—or was going to sell it to her. She may have placed it there on consignment."

"Velda says she bought it at an estate sale."

"Cindy bought it at an estate sale for Velda. I'm sure. You have to be careful with those two sisters. They're not honest. They cheat people whenever they can. That's been going on for years. I used to work for them about fifteen years ago when they owned a seafood shop. They screwed around with taxes a lot, claiming they paid employees higher wages than they did, using it as a deduction for themselves and then slipping the employees a couple bucks under the table to ignore what the W-2 forms said they made. They used to do things like that."

"Anything else ring a bell?"

"The weathervane does. I think that's on my list. The candlesticks may be. I'll check and let you know."

"Does your shop handle coins?"

"Not coins worth money, some old pennies and the like, but not coins for collectors."

"Any idea who does? Who would Cindy have sold a gold coin to?"

"No idea. Do you mind if I smoke? Or," she hastened to say, "I could step outside."

"No, that's okay. Go ahead. Did Cindy get along with everybody at the store?"

"Pretty much," she said as she tapped a cigarette out of a pack. "No one gets along with Jim Marsh. He's a cold fish. He's polite, but he's never nice. She got on with Kilpper pretty much. I know he actually liked her, even if he did yell at her sometimes. He yells at everybody."

"What about Ken?"

Charlotte frowned. "Ken's an asshole, you know. He works on the dock, loading and unloading. He's drunk half the time he's back there. He's leered at Cindy a few times. He leers at me periodically. I don't think it means anything."

"Any other guy she worked with who may have been interested in her?"

Charlotte took a long drag on her cigarette and thought. "Half the men who work there are gay, you know. We had a guy here last summer, Marshal, who was kind of sweet on her. He was a college student. He went back to college in Portland when the summer was up."

"Do you know if she was seeing anyone?"

"A guy, you mean? I don't think so. Nobody regular."

"Do you know anything about an antique Chinese sea chest Cindy sold by mistake and had to buy back?"

"Oh yeah. I know all about that. Kilpper ordered it special for a guy named West. Cindy sold it off the dock by mistake. She told Kilpper about it when he asked, of course. Boy did she get him in a bad mood. He blew his top. Serves him right. He didn't invoice it properly. We have a regular invoice procedure for items on special purchase. Kilpper skips it from time to time. Can't be bothered with the paperwork, I guess."

"Any idea who he bought the chest from?"

"Some guy from Turkey. He imports furniture through Hawaii."

"Turkey? He imports brass, and rugs, goods like that?"

"No. As far as I know, he sells furniture; chests, bureaus, cabinets, that sort of thing."

"I thought this sea chest was supposed to be Chinese."

"That's how it's listed in the books."

"Why is a guy from Turkey importing furniture from China for a guy in Oregon who has a shop in Hawaii?"

"Beats me."

"What's the name of this guy from Turkey?

"Omar Smith."

"Smith? You're kidding."

"Nope. That's what it says on the books."

"How odd."

"Probably not his real name."

"Do you know what happened to the chest?"

"No idea. Kilpper's pissed as all hell. He went down to that lawyer's office and raised a stink."

"What lawyer's office?"

"The one who took care of the legal matters after Cindy died."

"Brian Baer?" BJ asked, naming the attorney she had been working with on the estate. Since she was Cindy's heir, Baer was technically BJ's attorney, and he'd handled the estate matters for her while she was incarcerated.

"Yeah, him. Kilpper claimed they must have sold the chest or kept it instead of giving it back to the store. Of course he didn't say anything about the store having things it should have given back to Cindy's lawyer or paid for."

"Kilpper usually like that?"

"Yeah. He likes money. The store is run right. None of this marking up the product two-hundred percent and then calling it fifty percent off. He's great at sales, likes to handle the big stuff—you know, complete antique dining sets worth ten thousand dollars. That's why he's a partner. He can sell, but he can't manage the business. Can't do the paperwork. Any other questions?"

"You don't know what happened to Cindy's car, do you?"

"Her wagon? I have no idea. Have you talked to the police?"

"The police and the sheriff. They don't know what happened to it either."

"I don't suppose the sheriff was real helpful."

"No, he hasn't been. You know him?"

"Kinda, sorta, not really."

"What does that mean?"

"My second husband used to beat me up. Sometimes I'd call the police and sometimes I'd call the sheriff. Nobody did anything. Sometimes the police officer would make him go walk around the block to 'cool off.' The sheriff never did anything. One of the deputies finally told me that Carstair's policy was to make them wait twenty minutes before they came to a family disturbance call so it would it be all over by the time they got there."

"Been there done that," BJ said with a grimace.

"So I saw in the papers. One day it all came to a head. The son of a bitch, my husband, beat me up and gave me two black eyes using the butt of his hunting rifle. The next day I was so sore I could hardly get out of bed. I started my morning with a bottle of scotch, medicinal you know. That's what I called it back then."

"Why do men do this?"

"Because they can."

"Anyway, I spent the whole day drinking and hurting and swearing, and finally about four o'clock I was one pissed-off senorita, not to mention drunk off my butt. So I grabbed the hunting rifle and drove to his office and sat there in back waiting for him to come out to his car. He was going to get it right between the eyes, assuming I was sober enough to aim, which I wasn't. And do you know what?"

"You missed?"

"He had a heart attack in his office. Ambulance drove up and took him out feet first. He was DOA. I think somewhere in his subconscious he knew I was sitting out there waiting for him. The sheriff showed up because it was a slow day and finds me parked right by the back door with two black eyes and a rifle across my lap. He knew what was going on. Wasn't jackshit he could do about it, though, so I just got my happy ass home. We haven't had much to say to each other since then."

"That's quite the story."

"Yes, well, I better be getting home. Thanks for dinner. I'll find that list and let you know what the store's sold."

BJ saw Charlotte out and wished her goodnight. As she stood in the archway until Charlotte's car started, she noticed a red Honda parked down the block. When Charlotte had arrived, BJ noted that a small red Honda had pulled over and parked at the curb. BJ noticed it in particular because it looked like the ones The Laughing Sisters drove, but obviously must not have been them. BJ did not remember seeing it in the neighborhood before. She checked again before going to bed. The Honda was gone. Probably someone visiting one of her neighbors, she thought. Nothing to worry about. Odd that no one had gotten out of it while she was waiting for Charlotte to come up the stairs into the house, but probably, someone was taking the opportunity to check their phone.

CHAPTER SEVEN

Suspects

Saturday, BJ set off for McMinnville for an interview she dreaded, but she needed to talk to Bill Weathers, Cindy's ex-husband. She and Bill never had any major issues but didn't know what to do with each other. Bill came from an upper middle-class background and had no concept of the poverty BJ had grown up in. He'd been an impressive, if not exceptional, athlete and found his way in life paved by the quirky fact he was six-four and could hit eighty-eight percent of his free throws. He got into a university on an athletic scholarship even though his grades didn't qualify him for admission.

BJ, on the other hand, aced her grades in high school, but still didn't get scholarship money and worked her way through a two-year program over the course of five years. Once on the basketball team, Bill had gotten wined and dined by the local boosters, traveled all over the globe. He was given spending cash for traveling expenses that turned into crystal decanter sets and leather luggage, part-time jobs for full-time pay, and all his school expenses were picked up.

BJ, on the other hand, was kicked off the basketball team her senior year in high school when rumors got around that she was lesbian. When Bill finished college without getting a degree, a sports booster got him a job in a lumber mill in a management position with a base salary of thirty thousand bucks plus sizable commissions.

BJ got a degree in the trades with straight A's in class and managed to land an apprenticeship position, but she was harassed out of five consecutive jobs by men and ended up working moving furniture.

BJ's "radical" politics led to an arrest for joining a crowd who laid down on a train track in front of a train carrying arms to the El Salvador death squads. Meanwhile, Bill was so apolitical he had never voted.

The only thing they seemed to have in common was both being white and connected to Cindy. BJ was connected to Cindy *in spite* of being white, and Bill saw himself as connected to Cindy because he *was* white. Being a white boy paying attention to a black girl made Bill feel he was generous and unprejudiced, and BJ thought he probably assumed those qualities were what attracted Cindy to him.

BJ had different ideas about what Cindy found attractive in Bill. He was good looking, well built, and charming in his manner, but she suspected his carefree attitude toward life attracted Cindy. Cindy's father was an earnest man, deadly serious in all his endeavors, and he demanded that his children face a hostile world with the same amount of intense drive to succeed. Cindy was expected to apply herself in school, at home, and in church and to have fun only in ways that were constructive and designed to build character. Cindy found Bill's easygoing attitude a refreshing change.

They'd shared most family holidays, but BJ hadn't seen Bill since Cindy divorced him. They hadn't even communicated about Cindy's death. BJ had written Bill, asking for information, but he had not written back.

So BJ arranged this interview with Bill's second wife, Cathy, whom she'd never met and didn't really want to meet, but by gritting her teeth, she forced herself to go through with it. Finding correspondence in Cindy's desk that indicated Bill had stiffed her—or tried to—on the money due from the divorce didn't endear him to BJ either. But, speaking to Bill was necessary and she knew it.

Bill and Cathy lived in a new house in a cul-de-sac in a development outside of McMinnville. The house looked new and was split-level with a three-car garage and a fake stone facade on one side. The yard, about the size of a putting green, consisted of a ready-made lawn dotted with a few flowering trees and edged in hose-blown bark dust that hadn't been there long enough for a weed to grow yet. A Jeep Cherokee and Subaru Outback were parked in the driveway.

BJ rang the bell and was answered by a bleach-blonde woman in her late twenties holding an infant. Plucked eyebrows gave the woman an expression of surprise while the splash of blush on either cheek looked like a clown's rosy makeup. Ignoring the makeup, curled, colored hair, plucked brows, artificial lashes, and lipstick-altered shape of her mouth, BJ managed to conclude the woman's natural features were reasonably attractive.

"You must be BJ," she said in a neutral tone with a wan smile.

"Yeah, BJ McKay. Is Bill home?"

"He's around somewhere. I know he's expecting you. He's probably in the back. Come on in and have a seat." She escorted BJ into an overly furnished living room.

Sears must have had a sale, BJ thought uncharitably, taking a seat in one of the two matching checked swivel chairs.

"I'll go see if I can find Bill."

"Thanks."

Cathy was back a few minutes later minus the child. "Bill's out back. He'll be here in a sec. I'm getting him a beer. Can I get you one, too?"

"Yeah. That would be great." BJ realized they actually had a third thing in common, even if it was something as simple as both drinking beer.

Cathy returned with two open cans of Bud Lite. Well, BJ thought, maybe not that much in common since she drank Henry's and only from a bottle.

She thought Cathy was going to join her, but the woman set the beer down on a coaster near the couch and excused herself again. Bill came in the room as Cathy left it, plopped himself down on the couch, and took a swig of the beer.

"Hey, BJ good to see ya. How ya doin'?" he said with a false bonhomie that made BJ acutely aware of what a phony he was.

"The cops in Lincoln City are trying to find Cindy's car. Do you know what happened to it?"

"You mean her Volvo wagon?"

"Yes."

"No idea. Wasn't it at her house?"

"No. Cops don't know where it is. They say if it got tagged on the street as abandoned, the owner would have been notified. I don't suppose your name was still on the title, was it?"

"Nope. We bought the car at the same time I got my Jeep, but we had the titles separate. My name was on mine and her name was on hers."

"You never got notice from DMV or anything about it?"

"Nope. Are you sure the cops don't have it?""

"They say they don't. They're looking for it."

"Guy didn't ask me about it when he talked to me."

"What guy?"

"I guess he was the sheriff. Canon or something."

"Carstairs? Sheriff Carstairs?"

"Yeah, him."

"He talked to you?"

"Yeah. He came by my work. Right after it happened, like I was a chief suspect or something. Hey, you know me, BJ. I was pissed about the divorce and everything, but jeez, like I'd strangle somebody? That was four years ago. Come on. He may have thought I'd stolen her stuff."

"Really?"

"Well, maybe not stolen. He didn't accuse me of anything. They were missing a chest or something, and he seemed to have a real bug up his ass about it."

"A sea chest?"

"I dunno. An antique. You know I don't keep up with that."

"He asked you about it?"

"Uh huh. Did I pick it up for her? Did she leave it with me? Did I get it? He asked questions like that. Hey, I told him, we're divorced. I haven't seen Cindy since court. You know that went on a while, what with the long-term loan and Cindy being late paying me my share of the house and all. We had court appearances winding everything up, but geez, I got over her. I remarried for God's sake."

"Did he mention a guy named Edward West?"

"Nuh-uh. Wanted to know where I was, who saw me where, what my alibi was. He didn't talk about anything else."

"He didn't give you any idea who he suspected?"

"Besides me? Nope. He did ask about her boyfriends. I wouldn't know about that."

"Who do you think killed her?"

"I for sure didn't. I figure it was one of those sex things, you know. Hey, you know me. I don't even want to think about something like that, but what else could it be? All the loonies from California are coming up here these days."

"And he didn't ask you anything about the car?"

"Nope. He didn't say anything about cars. Just that chest."

"Did you know Cindy bought a gun?"

"Cindy? Buy a gun? You're shitting me."

"I found one in her house. You didn't loan it to her, did you?

"I don't' have any guns. And Cindy hated 'em. Are you sure?" he asked skeptically.

"She had a gun in the house, Bill."

"Maybe it wasn't hers."

"Who else would leave a gun there?"

"Nobody, I guess."

"Did she ever say anything about burglars?"

"Hey, we didn't talk. You know me. I didn't want any hard feelings, but you know we went our separate ways. The last time I talked to her was at court."

BJ asked a few more questions, but got no more information from Bill. They exchanged a minimum of pleasantries and BJ left. What she hadn't asked Bill, but would ask Lisa Carter, was whether or not Bill had an alibi.

Sunday afternoon BJ drove out to Mary and Vicky's for tea. Also invited was Detective Carter. The pouring rain made the drive miserable. BJ could hardly see the road. She got lost twice and had to backtrack before reaching the place. Even with only a few feet from the car to the door of the cottage, BJ got soaked before reaching it.

The cottage, in contrast to the weather, was richly inviting. A table was set next to the fireplace. The bungalow was cozily warm. Mary took her wet coat and settled BJ into the chair nearest the fire. Lisa arrived a few minutes later, and they gathered round the table for tea. Vicky brought an ancient silver pot to the table with matching milk and sugar jars and poured out strong, hot, *oolong* tea served with scones, dried fruit, brie and crackers, coffeecake, and petit fours with sherry for dessert.

When BJ expressed surprise at such a lavish spread, Vicky said, "In our house, tea isn't a beverage, it's a concept."

After some chatty conversation about the weather—an inescapable topic in Oregon—they turned to the subject of murder.

"We have a couple of things to report," Vicky said. "I know you probably know all this already, Lisa, but we're going to report it anyway to show our prowess as investigative reporters." She paused and picked up an old-fashioned spiral notebook from a table near the window and read from it. "Edward West was not unknown at the

Embarcadero. In fact, he stays there about every four months or so. He was down here in October of last year, July of last year, and early May or late April. He always gets the expensive rooms, the ones with wet bars for entertaining. He frequently eats at the restaurant even though he doesn't like seafood. He doesn't use the bar much. He keeps his own liquor stash in his room. He tips well. He's usually there during the week and stays for only three to four days, but he's been known to stay an entire week. He has a PO box in Neotsu.

BJ said, "Wow, you've found out a lot."

"And I'm not done yet. He's never known to have any female company, but business type executives come by the room. He has been seen in the company of Lester Walters, who runs a storage business in town, along with Jim Marsh, Steve Kilpper, Henry Crookam—he's an estate dealer—and Peter Bell. He's an attorney. Also, some visiting men my sources didn't know by name. He was into cars and had arrived in a Jaguar, a Lotus, an Alfa Romeo, and recently a Ferrari. He dressed well and wore expensive jewelry including a gold pocket watch, a Rolex watch, a diamond pinky ring, an emerald tie clip, gold cufflinks, and a ruby tie pin, but no wedding ring. He usually brought two extra suitcases but had large boxes delivered to the room and picked up by moving vans. He paid for everything in cash."

"I had some of that information, but not all of it. How did you manage it?" Lisa asked, sounding astonished.

"I can't tell you that. Trade secret. Just kidding. I know Kathy Vorhees. She works the desk there. I got her to invite me along to the weekly staff party. About a dozen of them get together Friday nights at the Sea Hag to hang out. Everyone wanted to talk about the murder. They all knew something about him, what he orders, what he brings, what he drives. They pooled their information, and I just listened."

"I'm impressed." Lisa helped herself to another petit four.

"But wait, there's more. He's got a shop in Hawaii, a shop in Seattle, as we all know, and bought merchandise through a shop in Portland called The Brass Candle, among other places. The Brass

Candle is closed. The owner is some guy named Gerry Ranson who got into trouble with the IRS over tax evasion. He was living high off the hog with a shop that wasn't making any money so someone got suspicious and turned him in. This Ranson guy disappeared from the scene and forfeited to the IRS several sports cars, including a Maserati, a luxury cruise boat, and three houses, one in Lake Oswego, one in Victoria, BC, and one in Newport. Ranson hasn't been traced, but rumor has it he went to Florida." Vicky flipped shut her notebook.

With a grin, Lisa said, "I knew about West's connection to Ranson, but I'll be damned if I can figure out how you found out."

"It's simple," Mary said. "We chatted with some of the salesclerks at his shop in Seattle. One of them is an herbalist, so we managed a rapport and she told us everything she knew. We found the rest using the Library's database which includes old issues of the Oregonian going back decades. The problems at The Brass Candle had been a nine days wonder and got lots of ink."

Mary said, "So West and Ranson were getting money from somewhere and probably laundering it through their business, or using the business for a front. Could be gambling, or prostitution, but my bet is drugs."

"Drugs coming in from Turkey via Hawaii," BJ added, "arranged by a man named Omar Smith."

"Who told you that?" Lisa asked.

"The bookkeeper at Bingham Antiques said West ordered a chest through a Turk named Omar Smith. Given that it's coming out of Turkey, we could guess the chest contains opium. Do you know anything about customs regulations?"

"Why?" Lisa asked.

BJ said, "I'm wondering if the chest is worth a great deal. Maybe instead of drugs, what if Ranson and West were smuggling rare antiques into the country, like museum pieces. I found a similar chest for sale in Portland for seven thousand dollars, but Cindy sold this one for about one tenth of that price. Let's suppose Ranson and West are buying antiques worth thousands of dollars and claiming they're worth a fraction of the cost in order to evade customs duties."

"It's possible," Mary said. "I find it hard to believe they could both get rich on what they saved on custom duties though. Unless they are smuggling in restricted articles or stolen items. That would explain why they were both hooked up with antique stores."

Lisa let out a sigh. "Sure would help to know where that damned chest was."

"Hmmm," Mary said thoughtfully, "if the chest is some sort of special antique, stolen from a museum, then there must be a buyer. West must have found someone who wanted to buy it before going to the risk of smuggling it into the country."

"That makes sense," Vicky said.

Mary went on. "Suppose the buyer found out that Cindy had it. It's easy enough to imagine how that happened. He demands the chest from West who explains Cindy sold it to the wrong person. The buyer tracks down Cindy, buys the chest from her, or more likely claims to be West's agent and picks it up. He kills Cindy to cover his tracks and later kills West. If the chest is worth thousands of dollars, hundreds of thousands of dollars, a one-of-a-kind item, and the buyer is part of a smuggling conspiracy, it might have been worth his while to save the money he planned on paying West and get rid of the witnesses to his crime."

BJ said, "People have committed murder for less, I suppose."

"Interesting ideas," Lisa said. "West probably did buy the chest for resale to someone, a collector or a drug dealer."

BJ asked, "You don't have any more information on her car, do you?"

"No. I talked to Carstairs but he doesn't have any leads on it. You didn't find out anything, I take it."

"I talked to Cindy's ex-husband, thinking it might be in his name still. He said a few interesting things. He didn't know where the car was, but Carstairs questioned him extensively about Cindy's murder."

Lisa said, "Husbands, estranged husbands, and ex-husbands are always considered chief suspects."

"He said he was asked for an alibi, but he didn't tell me if he had one. He also said Carstairs questioned him extensively about the chest, practically accused him of stealing it."

"What?" Lisa almost dropped her cup in her surprise. "Carstairs knew about the chest back then? That's incredible. I'm going to have to go have another talk with him. Did Bill say anything else of interest?"

"He said he hadn't seen or spoken to Cindy since court. Their last court date was early December when all they did was show up and agree they had each signed the most recent settlement document which resolved most of the unresolved property issues. But he was here in town last April. There's some correspondence in Cindy's desk about a Visa bill he was supposed to have paid after the divorce, and its years later and he still hasn't paid it. The letter refers to them meeting at the café in April. I talked to Kate, and she remembers it. She doesn't recall the exact date but she remembers around springtime last year."

"You three are better than an adjunct squad. I'll have to deputize you all and make you part of the force. Anything else I should know about?" Lisa asked, wiping up some tea she had spilled.

"I can't think of anything," Vicky said, pouring out the last of the tea. "But I can go over my notes and let you know later if that jars something loose from my memory."

"There's some shenanigans at the store but I think they're minor," BJ said. "Cindy bought some things for them, and they didn't pay her or reimburse the estate. That's not certain, yet, but I'll check. Charlotte gave me a list of items the store got from Cindy that she doesn't think the store paid for. I'll call the estate lawyer on Monday and double-check with him. Even so, we're only talking about a couple hundred dollars."

Vicky asked, "So you found everything on your scavenger hunt list?"

"Almost everything was sold to the store. Oh, except the things from the Rybakov estate sale. Cindy bought a solid Cherrywood antique tea cart for Velda Cox at the tea shop. I doubt that Velda ever paid her for it. I'll check with Brian Baer, the estate attorney, about that, too. That accounts for everything except the Ukrainian egg and a gold coin. I still haven't found them. The attorney for the Rybakov estate confirmed he sold them to Cindy, prior to the official sale, since she helped the guy running the sale with pricing. He was sure because Sallie asked for the egg and some other trinkets for the library, and they confirmed what had already been sold to Cindy. Cindy may have found out and given the egg or the coin to Sallie for the library. I'll ask Sallie about it. But Charlotte's list accounts for everything else."

Lisa held up a finger as she scrawled in her notebook. "You have all been very thorough."

"By the way," BJ said, "Velda Cox showed up a Bingham's a few days ago and threatened to kill Kilpper."

Lisa set down pen and notebook. "I know. We had an officer go by later and take a report. I spoke with Velda's sister, and she's going to get Velda to a doctor. This is some form of mental illness. She's supposed to be medicated for it, but isn't reliable about taking her medication. If it gets any worse, she may have to be institutionalized. She's fine when she's medicated."

"Hey," Mary piped up after several moments of silent thought, "I just had an idea. Is it possible that West and Ranson were selling the antique equivalent of bunk, so to speak? That's probably not the right term, but you know what I mean, don't you?"

"Yeah, I get it," Lisa said.

"I don't. What's bunk?" Vicky asked.

"Phony drugs," Lisa said. "You know, chopping up some oregano and selling it as marijuana."

BJ asked, "You think they may have been selling phony antiques, too?"

"I guess that would make sense." Lisa said. "Cindy must have had some way of coming up with a price for the chest when she first sold it. Logically, she looked at the invoice tag, saw the store's price was, say, five hundred and sold it for seven hundred. But what if West had found a buyer who would pay seven thousand for it? That might explain how he and Ranson were getting rich selling antiques."

"But I don't see how that would involve Cindy," Vicky said. "West would buy it back, and she'd have no idea who he sold it to or for how much. Besides, I can't see committing murder for antiques fraud. In these days of caveat emptor, it's probably not even illegal."

BJ said, "With immediate access to the Internet, 'let the buyer beware' is in full force. If people don't do their research, then it's their own fault."

"Right," Mary said, "Cindy wouldn't know who West was selling the chest to, but she could tell a fake. Antique fraud may not be that big a deal, but tax evasion is."

"That brings us back to West," Vicky said, "and he's dead."

Hesitantly, Mary said, "Maybe West killed Cindy and the buyer found out he was being duped and killed West. A criminal could be a likely buyer. He'd want the respectability of owning expensive things, but might not have the education to tell the genuine article."

"I wouldn't want to dupe a Mafia dude," BJ said.

Mary looked ready to argue. "West wouldn't know the buyer was Mafia. He probably figured he was *nouveau riche*."

"That's two killers tied up in one case," BJ pointed out. "Rather a lot, isn't it?"

Lisa said, "It's not as unlikely as you think. There are a lot more killers around than we know." She rose. "I need to get back to work. Thanks for the tea. You guys have been a lot of help. You really could be an adjunct squad."

"Just call us the Baker Street Irregulars," Vicky said.

Mary said, "We'll have to do this again sometime."

"Like next week," Vicky said, "so you can tell us how you're progressing with your investigation."

Lisa laughed.

"I'm not kidding," Vicky said with a smile as she escorted Lisa out.

Mary turned to BJ. "I'm backing the bunk theory. Vicky seems to like drugs as the motivation. Do you have a preference?"

"I'll take the smuggling museum pieces theory."

Vicky returned and seated herself. "We really ought to talk again this next week and keep each other up to date. I'm sure Lisa will have a busy week."

"What do you think she'll be doing?" BJ asked.

"If I were Lisa," Vicky said, "I'd talk to Lester Walters and see if West rented storage space from him, and if so, find out what's in it. Next I'd check the PO box he had at Neotsu. I'd also find out who the buyer was supposed to be for that chest. Maybe somebody at West's Seattle store would know. Charlotte might know more about Omar Smith. Then I'd find out what happened to Gerry Ranson."

"You do a pretty good job thinking like a detective," BJ said.

Sharply, Vicky said, "I think like an investigative reporter."

"Uh huh, right," BJ said with a wink. "I need to be going. JD will need a walk. Thanks for the tea. We'll have to do this again real soon,"

Sunday, BJ invited Kate out for dinner. "You cook all week long, let me take you out tonight," BJ offered.

Earlier that week, Brian Baer, the estate attorney, had sent BJ a check for several thousand dollars after locating a hitherto undiscovered savings account Cindy had at a small credit union, so BJ was feeling flush. She chose the Pier Five restaurant next to Bingham's Antiques. She'd noticed the place on her trips to the store and liked the ocean view and eclectic menu items.

At eight o'clock Kate showed up in a lovely clinging black cocktail dress and looked great.

"Doing business in town?" BJ asked.

"No. Why?" Kate asked as the server seated her.

"Wondered about the get-up is all."

Kate smiled. "That's because I got invited out to dinner at one of our better establishments."

She got dressed up for me, BJ thought. Whoa. Lucky me.

They started with a bottle of wine and fried calamari and went on to the entrees as BJ got Kate caught up on the discussion at the tea party. With the evening wearing on, BJ saw a planet on the horizon of the ocean where only the whites of the waves' crests could still be seen against the dark water and a few stars through the clouds.

"Lots of news on West," Kate said, "but anything new on your sister?"

"Yeah. I found out something very interesting. John Towerson is living in McMinnville."

"And he is . . . ?"

"Cindy's first husband."

"And I take it that he wasn't originally from McMinnville."

"He was from Seattle."

"And he's moved from a large city to a small town only a few miles away from where your sister lived."

"And less than half a mile from where Cindy's second ex-husband lives."

"Odd coincidence."

"If it is a coincidence."

"What is this guy like?"

"In my opinion, he's a self-righteous prick."

"You weren't on good terms with your first brother-in-law?"

"When he found out I'm a lesbian, he refused to have any contact with me. He tried to forbid Cindy to see me, but of course, she'd never go along with that."

"What is he doing in McMinnville?"

"He's got his own business there. He's a CPA."

"How'd you track him down?"

"Couldn't have been easier. I googled him. His business has a website and it lists his address."

"Any reason to think he's been here in town?"

"I'm checking it out. Hold on a sec." BJ reached around to her jacket hanging on the back of her chair and fished a snapshot out of her wallet

"I don't suppose he's been a regular at your restaurant."

"He's not a regular, but I couldn't swear that he's never been in. He's pretty average-looking. Has he remarried?"

"I don't know. I thought I'd hang out in McMinnville sometime this week and see what else I can find out about him."

"You be careful doing that."

"Oh, I'm careful."

"Say, that was something I wanted to ask you about, if you don't mind." Kate said, hesitantly, as she drank her coffee.

"What did you want to ask?"

"You were convicted, but you were out of prison in about five years. How come?"

"To tell you the whole story, my lawyer, who was court appointed, tried arguing self-defense, but Oregon law draws a bright line between self-defense that occurs in your home, and self-defense that doesn't. In Oregon, you have a duty to retreat unless the attacker is actually in your home, and Patrick wasn't. So, the facts were on my side, but the law wasn't."

"Okay, that makes sense. So what happened?"

"When Patrick first got violent, he threw things or punched the walls. Even when he graduated to hitting Susan, at first it was a slap or a push, not a full-out beating. The first time he actually beat her, she filed criminal charges against him. That was back in the day when you could do what's called 'civilly compromise' an assault case. My lawyer told me that when he was a greenhorn in the public defender's office, the easiest case to handle was a wife-beating. They always got charged with misdemeanors, and all he had to do was send his investigator out to the wife to sign the 'civ comp' papers and the case got dismissed."

"Uh oh, I can see the writing on the wall."

"Yes, Patrick convinced Susan he was going to change, see a therapist, and stop drinking, and he pointed out if he got convicted, his career in law enforcement would be ruined, so she got talked into dropping the charges. Then she divorced him, moved out, and got an FAPA—Family Abuse Prevention Act—restraining order. The first time he violated the order, he broke into her home and assaulted her, but the prosecutor only charged him with contempt of court for violating the order, not for the assault. He said they were easier to prove because it meant taking the case to a judge, not a jury, and all he had to show was that Patrick was at the house. He didn't need to prove injury like you do to make out a case of assault."

"But that sounds reasonable. I guess it didn't work though."

"Long story short, by the time I was on trial, Patrick had only one misdemeanor conviction for assault with no jail time, so the jury thought it must not have been serious. Susan testified on my behalf, and I testified, but two dykes against a police officer doesn't count for much. My lawyer tried to subpoena the doctor who treated Susan for her injuries at the last assault, but he didn't want to get involved. He kept evading service, so we couldn't get him as a witness."

"You're kidding. How cowardly. Sounds like you were in a real Catch-22."

"I was. The prosecutor's office, the same office that wouldn't go after Patrick for anything but restraining order violations because they said it wasn't necessary, argued there was no objective evidence showing Patrick was violent."

"He didn't have a history of that as a cop?"

"He did. He had more than his fair share of excessive force complaints, but the judge ruled they were irrelevant, and the jury never found out about them. The fact that he was a deacon in his church was admitted, as well as a citation for bravery he got as a cop, and his volunteer work with Special Olympics, but not his assaults on suspects. He frequently beat up women he charged with prostitution. I'm sure some shrink could make a few things out of that. But those are 'prior bad acts' and can't be admitted, unless I had known about them at the time and knowledge of those incidents had affected my decision to use deadly force. I knew he was violent, but I hadn't known about those specific complaints. So anyway, the jury came back with the verdict guilty of murder, but not first-degree murder since they found there was no premeditation."

"Why aren't you still in prison?"

"The maximum sentence in Oregon for second-degree murder is ten years. Oregon also does a sleight of hand with prison time. Judges know putting men in prison for long periods of time ends up being counter-productive, but the public wants to think people are going away for a long time, so you get sentenced to ten years, then you get one third off for what is called 'statutory good time.' You don't have to be good, its automatic. I also got credit for the time I was in jail, which was over two years before my case came to trial, so I was in prison for slightly less than five full years, but was incarcerated for over seven."

"What happened to Susan?"

"We were both getting a lot of death threats, probably from Patrick's buddies on the police force. Susan hid out in a battered women's shelter until she gave her testimony, and we agreed she needed to leave the country and not try to get in contact with me if I was convicted. The shelter got her out of the country. She's gone."

"Aren't you worried the cops will come after you?"

"A sort of funny thing happened at sentencing. After I was convicted, I had to see these people who assess risks and the convicted person's remorse and all that stuff. They make a recommendation about sentencing to the judge. I wasn't sentenced until three weeks after I was convicted. At my sentencing hearing, the wife of Patrick's precinct commander gave a suspiciously long and impassioned statement about what a loss to the community Patrick's death was. Some fellow cops figured out why she was so upset. She and Patrick had been having an affair. Most cops have fairly conservative morals and condemn affairs generally, but for a cop to be sleeping with another cop's wife is a big taboo, so all of a sudden, Patrick's friends weren't so supportive of Patrick anymore."

BJ finished the last of her coffee and decided to change the subject. "How's your friend in Portland?"

Kate picked up her cup and held it in front of her face, hiding her expression. With a shrug she said, "I don't have a friend in Portland anymore."

"Sorry to hear that."

"The server is looking at us like he's expecting us to leave."

"We have been here quite a while. I suppose we'd better get going." Looking at her watch, she was surprised it was almost ten o'clock. *My, how time flies when you're with a beautiful woman.*

As they were leaving the restaurant, BJ wanted to ask Kate to come by for a nightcap. *Are you kidding?* she thought to herself as she argued back and forth silently. *She just now told me she got dumped. She'll think I'm trying to jump her while she's on the rebound. Nonsense. That Portland relationship has been dead for weeks, if not months. But she only told me about it tonight. She's invited you over, twice, and dropped by a lot. It's time you took the initiative or she'll think you're not interested.*

But if I rush it, I could blow the whole thing. If we're headed that direction, we'll keep heading that direction. If you only shake hands good night when you get to the car, she'll conclude you're not interested, and it will hurt her feelings, considering she dressed up for you tonight. But if she feels rushed and uncomfortable, she won't be interested.

They walked around to the back of the building to the parking lot, and were abreast of BJ's car,

"Say, Kate, I don't suppose . . . that is, I was wondering—"

BAM

A gunshot shattered the stillness.

"That came from right around the corner," Kate said, sprinting off in that direction.

Must be her damned army training, BJ thought as she tried to jerk the keys out of her pocket. The keychain snagged on some fabric. She jerked harder. The keys stayed in her pocket. She pushed them down and away from the loose fabric and pulled on them again. They snagged again. She pushed them down further and ripped them off the knot of threads, finally managing to get them out of her pocket.

She shoved a key in the door lock. It wouldn't open. Wrong key.

She tried again and managed to unlock the car, open the passenger door, and grab the latch to the glove compartment. She pulled on it, forgetting she kept it locked and had to find yet another key to unlock it.

She grabbed Cindy's gun, chambered a round, and flicked off the safety. She turned on the flashlight function on her phone, and ran after Kate, around the back of the Bingham Antiques Building. She spotted Kate down at the far end, sweeping the light from her cell phone around the area.

"See anything?" BJ shouted, running to catch up.

"No, nothing."

Searching through and around all of the junk was slow going. Their cell phones gave off only narrow beams of low light. At the back of the building were a number of parked cars, a truck, a van, a pile of pallets, and odds and ends of discarded pieces of furniture.

Exterior lights from the restaurant came on when they got near the movement sensors and finally they had enough light illuminating the scene. A moment later, BJ heard sirens.

"There, near the loading ramp," Kate said, as a police cruiser pulled into the restaurant parking lot. BJ came over to see what she'd found. Right at the bottom of a ramp leading up to a loading dock was the sprawled body of Stephen Kilpper, shot right between the eyes.

CHAPTER EIGHT

Complications

The police didn't finish questioning BJ until nearly two a.m. The patrol officer who arrived when she and Kate found Kilpper's body took brief statements and had asked them to stay.

Lisa showed up about half an hour later. She checked in with them, explained it would be a while, and separated them. A state forensic team arrived about an hour after the shooting. Finally, Lisa took a more detailed statement from her, and BJ mentioned Velda Cox's threats. Lisa jotted everything down on an iPad. BJ had one bad moment when Lisa asked what she had wanted out of her glove compartment. Since being a felon in possession of a gun was a crime, which at that moment was in her jacket pocket, she said she thought she had a strong flashlight in the car. Lisa rolled her eyes in a "yeah, right" expression, but didn't pursue the subject.

Yawning with fatigue, BJ was finally allowed to go home. She didn't see Kate or Kate's Subaru and assumed she had already left.

So much for romance tonight.

On Monday, BJ, who slept in past her normal wake-up time, got a late start. Before going to Portland, she dropped by the library to return some books and asked Sallie about the egg.

Sallie said, "Now that you mention it, Cindy did volunteer to give us the egg once she found out about it. The value is nominal, but it's old and pretty. We thought it would be interesting for the library, along with a number of old photographs we picked up at the sale."

"Do you have the egg?"

"Actually, no. We never did get it. It seemed such a minor matter that I never wanted to bother the estate about it. Of course, we'd still be pleased to have the egg. If you don't want it."

"I haven't been able to find what Cindy did with it, but if I do, I'll let you know."

"Thank you very much. That would be kind of you. Do be sure and check out some books. Today's a good day to sit by the fire and read, the weather being what it is."

"Sounds good, but I've got some errands in Portland, so I'm driving up there for the day."

"Do be careful. The coast road can be treacherous in this weather."

"Say, you don't know anything about a gold coin Cindy picked up, do you?"

"A gold coin? An antique of some sort, I suppose. Doesn't the store know?"

"Apparently not."

"I'm afraid I can't help you there."

"Thanks anyway."

BJ stopped at the café for breakfast but Kate wasn't in. She figured Kate was probably sleeping in after last night. She grabbed a local paper, but the shooting happened too late to make it in. She checked her phone for local news, but the one report she found just noted that a shooting had taken place. The name of the victim was being withheld pending notification of next of kin. She knew more than this reporter did. That didn't help.

So far, she had never personally met her estate attorney, Brian Baer, but she'd managed to get an appointment with him. While BJ was in prison, they had arranged the representation and estate decisions by correspondence. Her closest contact with him previously had been picking up documents from his receptionist when she'd gotten out.

Brian was the complete opposite of the rural attorney, Vernon Cooper, who had handled the estate overall. Baer went in for progressive causes and only handled estate matters to pay the bills. He was in his mid-thirties, poorly dressed in a jacket that didn't match a tie that didn't match his pants or shoes. In spite of his liberal politics, as demonstrated by the picture in his office of him with Ralph Nader, he and BJ didn't get along well. She'd written him from prison begging for information and his contact had been aloof and unhelpful.

BJ found that many men, even left-of-center liberals, had a hard time dealing with a woman who had killed a man. Baer's correspondence was cordial, but hardly friendly. He managed the legal aspects of the estate competently, but with a number of delays due to his preoccupation with his other cases, the estate had not actually been settled yet. Even though BJ occupied the house and had received some cash advances against the estate assets, he had told her by phone that the final accounting was still many months away.

She arrived at his office five minutes early for her ten-thirty appointment, but he kept her waiting until eleven. After he finally ushered her into his office, he took a call and she waited another ten minutes. At long last, he put the phone down, straightened his tie, and shuffled the papers on his desk.

"The state department of revenue has approved the tax calculation we submitted. There has been a final inventory of assets and payment of claims. We should be submitting the proposed distribution to the probate department shortly and be in a posture to do a final distribution. Is that all you wanted to know?"

BJ explained the unpaid objects given to Bingham's antiques. She gave him Cindy's records of purchasing the items and the records she had received from Charlotte showing the store later sold them. Baer nodded periodically during her narrative and made notes, studied the file and nodded some more. He did not make eye contact with her once.

When she finished, he said briskly, "Good job bringing this to my attention. I'll put in a claim right away and get you this money. Thanks to the documentation you've given me, there won't be any problem with it." He stood up to usher her out.

BJ remained seated. "The store never sent you any money, did they?"

"Oh no," he said. "I'm sure they haven't."

"And Velda Cox hasn't either?"

"No. But I'll get it, don't worry."

"I understand Steve Kilpper got in touch with you about a sea chest he wanted back."

Baer's face flushed a deep red and he slowly sat down. "Yes, he did. He wasn't tactful either. He claimed it belonged to the store, repeating that Cindy was unlawfully in possession of it, emphasis on 'unlawfully,' which, of course, isn't true."

"Was it? In her possession, I mean."

"Not that I was able to ascertain. I went down to her house with him and went through it and we didn't find any chest such as he was describing."

"Did you find a Ukrainian Easter Egg or a gold coin while you were looking through the house?"

"We were only looking for a chest. Why do you ask?"

BJ explained about the list and the two missing items.

Baer shook his head. "I don't know anything about those."

"Thanks for your time."

"I'll get that money from the store. Don't worry."

"Thanks."

After BJ left Baer's office, she drove downtown to a shop in Morgan's Alley that handled rare coins. In the estate appraisal records Vernon Cooper had sent her, she found a description of a gold coin and a notation of sale to Cindy. The description wasn't helpful, it stated only "gold (?) very tarnished coin, bust on one side, eagle on reverse, unreadable lettering near the bottom of eagle," followed by dimensions in metric measurements, which she guessed made it larger than a quarter but smaller than a fifty-cent piece.

She showed the coin dealer the description of the coin and asked him about it. He indicated he wasn't familiar with it, but would check. He spent nearly half an hour thumbing through catalogues and finally told her he couldn't find any American coin fitting the description. He referred her to another coin shop which handled foreign coins.

The proprietor of this shop also tried to be helpful, but he only carried current coins, no antiques. But he told her if it was gold and old, it was probably worth a tidy sum. He didn't know of any dealer who might handle such coins.

While she was in Portland, BJ had tried to find Cindy's contact, Lucy, but a note on the shop door indicated that Lucy was in the bush in Alaska on a buying expedition and out of range of cell phone communications.

Her attempt to track Lucy led her to the antique stores on Hawthorne Street just past two in the afternoon, and she still hadn't had lunch.

Putting her investigation work aside, she walked down to Cup & Saucer Café, decided on the pheasant in orange sauce, and ordered a light wine to go with it. She was sipping meditatively when a man's voice said behind her in soft, but deliberate tones, "Isn't alcohol a violation of your conditions of parole?"

BJ stood and turned, finding herself eye to eye with the man who prosecuted her. He had refused to offer her a deal because she'd shot a police officer. He tried as hard as he could to get a jury to convict of her first-degree murder for a life sentence.

"I'm not on parole," she said, standing toe to toe with him. "I did straight time. And it's none of your business."

He still kept his voice low. "It makes me sick that you're walking the streets when a good man is dead."

"If your office had put that good man in jail after he broke my arm, he wouldn't be dead now, would he?" She took a step closer so she was only a few inches away from his face. She clenched her hands into fists, wanting desperately to hit him, knowing that would send her back to jail.

"Shot any other officers recently?" he baited.

"I only shoot cops when they come gunning for me. You knew Patrick Hunter was a wife-beater. You knew he was a bad cop. He was under investigation when I shot him, so why did you back him up by coming after me with a first-degree murder charge?"

"Patrick Hunter was a Marine."

"So?"

"I was a Marine. We take care of each other. You know why it's a man's world, and you girls don't run it? Because men understand loyalty. Oh, and I hope you've learned your lesson, because you try anything again, and you'll go to prison for the rest of your life."

BJ stepped back but didn't look away. Had she learned her lesson? She didn't regret spending seven years in prison to protect Susan from Patrick, but now, more than anything in the world, she wanted to make sure she never, ever went back, not for any reason. She certainly couldn't see sticking her neck out just to be loyal to another woman.

He backed away, his face twisted with hate. Before he got to the door, he paused, gave her a middle finger, and mouthed the words, "Semper Fi."

Always loyal? That's what the Marine Corp motto "Semper Fi" meant. She didn't think Patrick deserved much loyalty or devotion. He'd brought about his own destruction.

She sat back down to her lunch, but found it had lost all its taste.

On her way back to the coast, BJ drove through McMinnville. She plotted a GPS route on her phone to locate Towerson's house. Driving around McMinnville and seeing how it was laid out, she decided Towerson's closeness to Bill made sense. Only one area of town was "suburban" for the newly affluent who were buying homes.

Towerson had a huge three-story, two-garage home and the landscaping indicated it was only a few years old. One of the doors was open, and BJ saw three children's bicycles inside along with a minivan. Typical American family, she thought. Though, given John's religious beliefs and opposition to birth control, she was surprised he didn't have more kids. Maybe he hadn't been married long enough to have more.

While BJ was sitting in her idling car, a young woman came out of the house, got in the van, and backed out of the garage. Having nothing else to do, BJ followed her into town. She stopped at a church which advertised a daycare, walked inside, and came out a short while later with five children, two of them toddlers who were too young for bikes.

BJ got a good look at Towerson's new wife. She appeared to still be in her late twenties. She must have had her first child in her late teens, BJ thought. And by now, Towerson must be pushing forty. He'd been a slightly older than Cindy when they'd married. With Cindy, BJ knew he'd felt superior because he was white. Now he seemed to be basing that need for superiority upon age. With a new wife to push around and lord it over, BJ wondered if he still needed to brood about Cindy. Still, he was now living less than forty-five miles away from where she'd been killed.

Before leaving town for the coast, BJ cruised by Towerson's business, a refinished Victorian home looking impressively prosperous in the old center of town. He didn't seem to be sharing the building with any other business. BJ saw a Jaguar parked in back and jotted down the plate number.

Once back at the coast, she picked up JD from Vicky's and got home around six. Sekhmet was acting odd—restless and upset. Checking around the house, she didn't find anything amiss. She went outside and walked around to find plants trampled near the back door and lower windows. Though Mary and Vicky had picked comfrey from this area, BJ was sure the dirt had not looked like this before. They'd been very careful not to flatten anything. Someone had tried to get into the house again but was foiled by the new locks.

She got the gun from the car before locking up for the night. She felt concern about having a gun in hand, especially after the close call at the Kilpper crime scene. But better safe than sorry was her rationale.

Tuesday, BJ drove to the junkyard in search of Cindy's car. The yard in question was the only one in the county, tucked behind the town and backed by an exhausted quarry. Two wobbly fences of corrugated steel were placed around the two sides facing the road, leaving a gap of some size between where the rock sides of the quarry met the steel. BJ assumed the fence was for aesthetic purposes since the odd cut of the land kept it from actually keeping out anyone or any vehicle. BJ imagined it as an invitation to anyone who wanted to steal car parts or to the local teenagers who wanted some privacy.

She found Alfred at the office building next to the gate. He appeared to be in his late sixties. His clothes were worn, but neat and clean. He was clean-shaven except for a carefully trimmed mustache and wore his hair short. BJ explained her errand.

He nodded with understanding. "We have to keep careful records of cars because of all the car thieves." He pulled an oversized black ledger from the desk drawer. "You see, this is it." He opened the book and showed her the page. In neat, legible script he entered dates received, vehicle plate data, the VIN, the name and address of the person or company bringing in the car, and the date the report went out to DMV of the arrival.

The records seemed meticulously kept and detailed. BJ thumbed through the book and found no evidence of an entry being deleted anywhere.

"You do this for every car?" she asked.

"Every time a car goes through that gate, I put it in the book."

"Thanks for letting me check."

BJ left the office and strolled back over to her car. Cindy's Volvo wasn't going to be there, then. She believed Alfred when he said he noted every car going through the gate. His statement gave her an idea. She walked down along the line of the fence and examined the gap between it and the rock wall of the quarry. The hole was big enough for someone to drive a car through. She hiked along the rock wall, climbed up a slope of crushed rocks and broken tree limbs, and looked over the lot. She spotted a likely vehicle and hiked back down to the junkyard.

Getting to the car was a chore. She crawled up and over a couple of mangled vehicles before reaching it. The windows had been smashed out, but there was almost no body damage. Once there, she pulled a slip of paper out of her wallet that had the VIN number on it. As heir, she'd gotten an inventory of known property from Brian Baer which had included the VIN, and she'd written it down before she'd started her hunt. Like a contortionist, she stuck her head through the broken driver's side window so she could read the number.

The VIN matched. She had found it, Cindy's car. Heart beating faster, she almost couldn't believe her good luck.

Other than the smashed windows, the Volvo seemed undamaged. BJ peered into the interior, hoping the chest was in the back, but no such luck.

She returned to the office to inform Alfred of her discovery.

First Alfred's face went red, then he stood there shaking his head, as penitent a man as she'd ever seen. "I'm awful sorry, ma'am. Really, truly, I didn't know."

"I get it."

He kept shaking his head as if perplexed beyond his ability to handle the news. "Ma'am, I don't know how in tarnation that happened. Really, I—"

"Yeah, yeah, it's not your fault. Don't worry about it. Tell you what. Please call over to the detective, and let's get her out here to look."

Detective Lisa Carter arrived ten minutes later and clambered over the old heaps to reach the scuffed-up Volvo while BJ explained how she had found it.

"Did you open the doors, or enter the vehicle?" Lisa asked.

"No. I looked in the windows up front to check the VIN and looked in back, but didn't actually touch it."

Lisa nodded her approval.

"What happens now?"

"Carstairs will be here with a forensic team in a few minutes."

"Carstairs?"

"It's still his case."

"I suppose forensic will go over it for fingerprints."

"Fingerprints, fibers, bloodstains, semen stains, the whole routine."

"Do you get to see those reports or do they only go to Carstairs?"

"I'll get to see them, don't worry."

"As the heir, do I get a copy of the inventory of the car's contents?"

"Yes. I can send it to you."

"Thank you. Any arrests yet on Kilpper's murder?"

"We talked to Velda Cox, and her sister Theodora says they were home together all evening."

BJ frowned. She doubted the sister's word could be trusted. "Any reason to think Velda has a gun?"

"She doesn't have a concealed carry permit—which doesn't mean she does or does not have a gun. Her sister says she doesn't, though."

"Her sister seems to be helpful."

"I've noticed."

"Since Carstairs is on his way," BJ said, "I think I'll get out of here. I don't think that man likes me much."

Lisa nodded. "I'll be in touch about what we find."

"Thanks. Oh, by the way, I found John Towerson."

"That was Cindy's first husband, wasn't it? Where did you find him?"

"In McMinnville, with a new wife and five children."

"McMinnville, huh? That's pretty close."

"My thoughts exactly. I wonder why he ended up down here. He's from Seattle."

"Odd," Lisa said. "Why would he move?"

"Maybe you could ask him."

Wednesday of that week BJ met with Brian Baer and Jim Marsh to discuss the items missing from Cindy's estate. The meeting took place at Marsh's office which was located in downtown Ocean City, not at the antique store. The downtown office was in a modern building, for the town, and the only one that could be described as pretentious. Marsh's co-tenants included several lawyers, an accounting firm, and some insurance companies. The carpet was plush, and the furniture was Oriental with a few nice antiques. A bleach-blonde secretary guarded the inner sanctum, multitasking at a desk with both the reception and secretarial equipment.

BJ and Baer entered Marsh's office together. They found Marsh waiting for them. This was BJ's first view of him. Jim Marsh looked like a typical businessman who was moderately successful. In his early fifties, he had nondescript brown hair, wore a dark blue suit, and was clean shaven and somewhat hefty. He seemed cordial and reticent in his manner. After shaking hands all round, BJ sat back to let Baer conduct the meeting.

In contrast to Marsh, Baer looked as if he got his clothes from a Saint Vincent de Paul thrift store. He wore a pair of blue corduroy pants, brown loafers, a white shirt one size too big, and a tan coat and blue-striped tie that didn't match anything else, especially not his socks, one of which was dark blue, the other black.

BJ wasn't expecting much from him, but Baer put the case clearly and succinctly. He presented Marsh with copies of Cindy's canceled checks for the purchased items, her bank account records showing an absence of comparable deposits, and copies of the store's inventory list from Charlotte showing the store had received the items. Without being at all accusing in his manner, he explained the store would have to reimburse the checks so that the estate could clear probate.

Marsh hemmed, hawed, and repeatedly said he'd "have to check into it" and "can't say right now."

Baer remained firm. "I need to receive the money within ten days, or I'll be forced to file a claim against the store to get it."

Marsh harrumphed a few times, but Baer wouldn't back down. He insisted once again on the full amount within ten days or a lawsuit. "If you want to check the books, you should do that now. Ms. McKay and I will wait."

Marsh excused himself from the office for a few minutes to "check the books." Ten minutes later, he reappeared and handed Baer a check.

BJ wondered why he had made the decision to cough up the funds, but Marsh's demeanor gave her no clue. Baer thanked him and escorted BJ out of the office. She thought it was pretty good work for a man who couldn't match his socks.

For no specific reason, BJ drove by the tea shop while on her way home. Parked in a spot marked "reserved for owner" was an older model red Honda, like the one she'd seen outside her house during Charlotte's visit. BJ didn't like what that was adding up to. Was she being stalked by a crazy woman? Velda Cox had no issue with her, but crazy people were notoriously irrational. She remembered the woman staring at her in the restaurant. She'd found it unnerving then. Of course, lots of people drove red Hondas There was no reason to think the one parked outside her house the night Charlotte had been there was Velda's. But still . . .

On Thursday, BJ decided to drop by John Towerson's office and see what, if anything, he had to say to her. She arrived just before ten and announced herself to the receptionist who passed her name on to Towerson, and he instructed the receptionist to show her back to his office. She surmised he wouldn't remember her name, or he would not have agreed to see her.

He didn't appear to recognize her, but it'd been over fifteen years since he'd last seen her and that had been, at most, half a dozen times. She remembered *him* well enough. He was a small man, not any taller than BJ, still thin, and clean shaven with heavy horn-rimmed glasses. She remembered the tight line at his mouth that gave him a perpetual look of having bit into a lemon. He'd had a lot more hair when she'd seen him last.

"And what can I do for you, young lady?" he asked with a grimace that was an attempt at a smile.

"I wondered how long it's been since you've seen Cindy," BJ said, getting right to the point.

"Cindy?"

"Your ex-wife."

His expression changed immediately, now quite surly. "She was never my wife. The marriage was annulled."

"How long has it been since you've seen her?"

"Years."

"I find that hard to believe, seeing as how you're only about forty-five miles apart."

"I have no idea where Cindy is and do not care. And I don't know who you are or why you'd be asking. If this is an attempt to get money, it won't work."

"You're not interested in seeing her again?"

"Not in the least. Now if that's all, perhaps you'll let me get back to work now."

"So you don't know?"

"Don't know what?" His eyebrows raised in query and BJ saw he now recognized her.

"Cindy was murdered."

His eyes widened and he looked a little flustered, but he corralled his emotions and said, "I can't say I'm surprised that she came to a bad end. Now please leave my office."

"How did you end up in McMinnville from Seattle?"

"My wife is from here. We moved into her parents' home after they died, not that it's any of your business." He rose, red-faced, and waited for her to leave.

BJ thought it looked like he was still holding a grudge without ever having anything to be aggrieved about, and he was oddly uncurious about a murder. Not to mention very defensive.

Before leaving town, BJ checked the newspaper morgue in downtown McMinnville and found Cindy's murder had made the front page and then for several days running appeared in the metro section.

Odd that Towerson had missed it . . . if he were telling the truth.

Sunday BJ was back at Mary and Vicky's for tea again. So was Detective Carter.

"That was smart work finding Cindy's car." Lisa's compliment was warm, and BJ felt pleased with herself.

"Seems to me," Mary said, "the person who hid the car must have extensive criminal experience to think of that trick."

Vicky said, "Not necessarily. You could read about that in a book."

"I thought the layout of the property sort of suggested the idea," BJ said.

Mary nodded. "Which would mean the person who junked it there knew the layout, most likely a local—and probably a longtime local."

"Find anything in the car?" BJ asked Lisa.

"The full reports aren't in yet, but the lab did find evidence that the murder took place in the car."

"Whoa. So Cindy was in the car with the killer?"

"Yes. The lab evidence shows she was in the driver's seat at the time she was killed. The autopsy report found scrapings of black leather underneath her fingernails matching scratch patterns in the black leather wheel cover in the car. Or," Lisa rolled her eyes, "at least that was what someone in forensics leaked to the press."

Her sister had been strangled by the passenger in her own car, someone she had trusted. BJ felt a deep swell of anger thinking about what Cindy had suffered. "Must have been someone Cindy knew."

"Presumably. Unless she gave a ride to a stranger."

"Cindy didn't give rides to strangers," BJ said. Her sister wasn't the sucker type who went around helping people on the side of the road. She was much too cautious for that. "Did you find anything else in the car?"

"Some fibers and hairs that haven't matched up with anything yet. No fingerprints except Cindy's. The fibers may prove critical if we get a suspect, though."

Vicky said, "I suppose you checked them against West's hair?"

"Yeah, we did. They didn't match. We don't have any reason to think West was in the car. But in addition to proving Cindy must have known her killer, the killer has to know something about forensic evidence to hide the car and let any evidence degrade. Wasn't anything else in it. With the windows broken out letting in the elements, we weren't able to recover much."

"Which points to an experienced criminal," Mary argued.

"Or a well-read one," Vicky suggested.

BJ asked, "Turn up anything else on West, yet?"

"We found out he did rent storage space in town, which someone apparently broke into recently. There's nothing in it now. We also checked his post office box. Nothing in that either, but the post office will hold any future incoming mail for me. So far, nothing has come in for him."

Mary scooped up a cookie from the plate on the table. "What do you mean the storage space was 'apparently' broken into?"

"Dust marks on the floor show large items were stored there, probably furniture and boxes. Seems unlikely someone broke in and moved things around. Several houses look over the area. If someone was moving furniture in the dead of night, it's unlikely it would go unreported by the neighbors. My own theory is that someone else had a key. He, or she, moved the items in broad daylight and then came back and jimmied the lock to make it look like a break-in."

"Find anything other than dust marks?" BJ asked.

"Scuffed footmarks. Not enough to get a print, but we did find a fingerprint. It doesn't belong to the staff or West. We ran it through the computer, and it doesn't belong to anyone with a record, either. May not mean anything, might turn out to mean everything."

"Sounds like you're making progress."

"Oh, some."

Vicky said, "I don't suppose Gerry Ranson has turned up."

"As a matter of fact, he has, so to speak. In Hawaii. He's dead. Drowned while swimming. Accidental death. We got the death certificate from the Department of Vital Statistics. He died about a year ago."

"The plot thickens," Mary said. "Awful if you had to go to Hawaii to investigate, particularly this time of year when the place is so full of tourists."

Lisa smiled. "The police in Hawaii are looking into things for us and don't need my assistance, unfortunately."

"Do the police have anything on Towerson?" BJ asked.

"All I can tell you is that he doesn't have a criminal record of any kind, not even a traffic offense. Have you talked to him, BJ?"

"As a matter of fact, yes, I did. He didn't have a lot to say to me."

Lisa asked, "What's he doing in McMinnville?"

"He said his wife is from there. He met her in Seattle, and when her folks died, she inherited a house, so they moved here. The house they live in looked pretty new to me, at least the landscaping did, so I doubt that was the parent's house. They may have inherited enough money to buy it or he's doing well as a CPA or some of both."

Lisa nodded. "Did he know how close he was living to Cindy?"

"He says not. He says that he didn't know that she was dead. He said he hadn't thought about her since the annulment."

"Did you believe him?" Mary asked.

"No." In her opinion, Towerson was afraid of something. Maybe he'd never told his wife about Cindy. He wasn't very forthcoming about anything, and his lack of sympathy for his "ex" was stunning.

"I've got to be off," Lisa said, standing up. "Thanks again for tea."

"Suppose she told us everything?" Vicky queried after Lisa left.

"Doubtful," Mary said. "Professional reticence, not compromising an investigation, all that."

"I'm surprised she told us what she did," BJ said.

Vicky said, "I'll bet that half of that makes the papers tomorrow. The storage owners must have known about the break-in or apparent break-in, and I'll bet the post office staff is all talking about the hold on the PO Box."

Vicky turned to BJ and gave her the eye. "You're not holding out on us, are you?"

BJ grinned. "Of course not. I haven't found out anything interesting. I still haven't found the egg, or the gold coin, which is probably pretty valuable. Cindy paid a hundred dollars for it which might have been less than the value of the gold content. If it turns out to be an antique Russian coin, it could be worth a lot of money. When I was in Portland, I got the name of a dealer in Russian antiques, but she's out of state right now. I'll have to wait until she gets back to talk to her. In the meantime, I have to wonder where the coin is."

"Something like that is so small," Vicky said, "it could be hidden anywhere."

"I got my money back from the store." She described the meeting she and Baer had with Marsh.

"What did you think of him?" Mary asked.

"Hard to draw any conclusions."

"Given the fact his partner was just murdered, I'm surprised he's even back on the job so soon."

"I'd take a few days off from work if my partner was murdered." BJ said. "But Velda Cox only made threats against Kilpper, so maybe he figures he's safe. Baer is going to call Velda this week and get her to pay for the tea cart. I told him about her rages, and he promised to be careful."

"She was back at work Friday," Vicky said. "I went in and bought some loose tea for today. She seemed a bit fuzzy and distracted, but sane."

BJ asked Vicky, "Does she own that old red Honda that's parked in their lot?"

"The one that looks like mine? Yes. Why do you ask?"

"One like that was parked up the block from my house when Charlotte came over. I wondered if someone had followed her from the store."

"Could be, but I doubt it. Every fifth person in town owns a Honda, and half of them are red," Vicky pointed out.

BJ had indeed noticed a large number of similar red Hondas.

"Got anything planned for this week?" Mary asked.

BJ shook her head. "I'll do some thinking. I'm waiting to see if Lisa turns up anything else on the car contents."

"What I don't understand," Mary said, "is why Cindy was killed in the car at all. The killer must know evidence would be left in the car, so why kill her there?"

BJ said, "My theory is that the killer needed the car to transport Cindy's body. Less risky than the killer using his own car."

Vicky nodded. "That would make sense."

On Wednesday, BJ and Brian Baer met with Velda Cox about the antique tea cart. She seemed a different woman from the one at Bingham's who had been screaming. BJ noted that Velda was neatly dressed in something close to a business suit, skirt, blouse and jacket, with pearls and matching earrings. Her gray hair was up in a French braid, a seemingly functional and rational businesswoman; enough of a business woman to not like to part with any money. At first, Velda swore absolutely she had not bought the cart from Cindy. When confronted with the auctioneer's records, she changed her mind and admitted she bought it *through* Cindy, but then swore she had paid for it.

As Velda and Baer argued the point, BJ examined Velda's affect carefully. Her face had a blank look with almost no change in expression, her emotions eerily flat, but quite coherent. BJ was almost certain the lack of facial expression or modulation in voice tone was the result of medications. Her impression was that Velda was sane, a brazen liar, but a sane one. When Baer demanded to see the canceled check, Velda claimed she didn't keep any. Baer threatened to get her bank records, at which point she grudgingly admitted the possibility of the check being lost and wrote Baer another one.

"Do you see much of Charlotte, these days?" BJ asked casually as Velda put away her checkbook.

"I don't know what you mean," Velda snapped, suddenly animated. "I don't know any Charlotte."

"Charlotte," BJ prompted, "who used to work for you when you owned a seafood place."

Velda said, her voice rising, "I do not know any Charlotte Gibson, and I don't intend to answer any more questions."

BJ decided it would be a bad idea to antagonize the woman who had no trouble remembering Charlotte's last name. She wondered if Charlotte was also on the woman's hate list and if Velda had been following Charlotte. She sure seemed upset at the name. BJ decided she had better warn Charlotte and tell Lisa about it.

After leaving the tea shop, Baer gave BJ a manila envelope stuffed with random bills from creditors and paperwork relating to the estate that he thought she should look at. He had paid out a lot of Cindy's bills and wanted BJ to check through them. She promised she would.

Once back at the house, BJ sat down at the roll-top desk to sort through the bills Baer had given her. Fortunately, Cindy kept neat records, making it easy to cross-reference debts paid and unpaid. She owed some outstanding credit card amounts for department stores, medical bills of a minor nature, a dental bill, car repair bill, and regular utility charges.

BJ also turned up an invoice from some place called Second Time Around for storage. She had no idea what that was about. The address on the billing showed the store was in town. She decided to check it out.

Second Time Around was in an area located at the south end of town, which consisted of several rambling buildings on a lot next to a gas station. The note on the door indicated it would be closed until Friday due to owner absence. BJ peered through one of the dirty windows and spotted mostly garage sale junk. Didn't look like the type of place Cindy would be associated with, but she might have used it for her treasure hunting. BJ decided to come back Friday to check out the storage bill.

CHAPTER NINE

The Second Time Around

Friday the Thirteenth dawned cold and clear. BJ took the dog out for a jog on the beach and then drove down to the café for breakfast. Kate fixed her a full meal of ham steak, eggs, hash browns, a fruit bowl and black molasses bread. BJ was on her fourth cup of coffee when the crowd thinned out enough that Kate had a moment. She took off her apron, poured herself a cup of coffee and joined BJ in the booth near the door.

"Your ex-brother-in-law Bill was in here not too long ago."

"Not too long ago as in when?"

"Last Monday."

"Really?" BJ raised her eyebrow quizzically. "Any idea why?"

"Something about the chest, I gather. He was in here having lunch with the sheriff, and I overheard them mentioning it a couple of times."

"Oh, yeah? And how's Sheriff Charisma?"

"Not too good from the look of things. I didn't catch that much of the conversation. I stay pretty busy behind the counter. Bill looked the same, attentive, but not worried. Wasn't in a great mood, but didn't seem put out. Sheriff was tense."

"With the Sheriff, how can you tell? To me, he always looks tense."

"He's a regular. I can get a read on his moods. Whatever was bothering him wasn't anything he wanted to share. Lisa came in while he was here, and they both ducked out without saying anything to her."

"Professional rivalry?"

"If so, that's new. They usually get on pretty well."

"Speaking of Bill, are you sure he was down here last Spring?"

"Yeah. I remember he and Cindy were sitting in the booth near the counter, and it was so hot we had to open that window for the first time since September. I had to get Bill to help me with it."

"What kind of mood was Bill in then?"

"Pretty upset as I recall. He sounded argumentative. Hadn't been able to get ahold of Cindy because she'd been helping with the Rybakov estate. He was upset. They had some papers to sign about the divorce, something about not being able to transfer title before taxes."

"So around April fifteenth, if they're talking about taxes."

"I guess so."

"Thanks. I'll pass this on to Lisa."

"I didn't get a chance to thank you for dinner the other night," Kate said with a smile.

"We were rudely interrupted, as I recall."

"I appreciate it. I had a good time—until we got to the parking lot."

"We'll have to try again sometime." BJ finished the last drop of coffee, put a few bills down on the table. Kate gave her a flirtatious wink as she left.

Second Time Around was a fifteen-minute walk from the café, so BJ left her car at the café lot. As she approached, she saw the place was doing a brisk business for a Friday morning. Tourists were already coming in from Portland and stopping. The lot was conveniently located at a junction of three highways near the river. BJ stepped inside the main building, which looked like a converted garage, and browsed. Second Time Around indeed, she thought. More like the hundred-twenty-second time around.

The store was a hodge-podge of unsorted junk piled everywhere. Tables were loaded with what looked like rejects from garage sales. A lot of junky furniture was crowded into groupings between the tables, mostly old sofas and end tables. These types of goods were not antiques, and the store didn't seem the type Cindy would associate with.

Eventually, BJ worked her way around to the proprietress who was busily doing a hard-sell to two tourists contemplating the purchase of a pair of Elvis paintings on black velvet. After ten minutes of creative haggling, the paintings were sold for what BJ thought to be a ridiculously high price.

The proprietress was a woman who looked fifty going on eighty. She wore a peculiar dress that resembled a grey-flannel muu-muu. "Whatcha lookin' fer, honey?" the woman asked, as she approached BJ. "You tell me, and I got it some place."

"I came about this billing invoice." BJ handed her the paper.

"Finally. I've had that damn chest here nearly a year. Been sending bills to the lawyer for months. How come he ain't paid it?"

"I can pay you now."

"You got papers saying it's your chest? You ain't Cindy. I know that. I ain't giving it to just anybody. You gotta have papers."

"I've got papers showing I'm the heir to the estate."

"Is it signed by a judge?"

"Well, no."

"You want that damn chest you gotta show me papers signed by a judge. I ain't gettin' in the middle of no lawsuit. Nobody what ain't got papers signed by a judge is getting' that chest, not a lawyer, not the sheriff, not you."

"The sheriff has been by?"

"Yep. Came here first thing this morning. I told him the same I'm telling you. Don't care if I get some receipt or not. I gotta have papers signed by a judge to give anybody that chest."

With all the emphasis on signed papers, BJ thought the woman was starting to sound like a parrot. Patiently she asked, "Did the sheriff say when he'd be back?"

"Said next week."

"I'm not sure we're talking about the same chest. Mind if I see it?"

"You thinkin' I don't have it? Hell, it's still there. Come on back and I'll show ya."

The proprietress led BJ to the back of the store, pausing to yell to someone named Florie to watch the till for a moment. They went outside the main shop to a dilapidated shed behind it. The shed, listing somewhat to port, was accessible by two stout but old doors. The woman pulled an old-fashioned key out of a pocket, unlocked the doors and swung one open. The interior was dimly lit by some dirty casement windows at the back. The woman turned on a switch for an overhead light, and they walked in. BJ's first thought was to look at the roof for water leaks, but it appeared sound.

"There it is, right there, the woman gestured, "like the day she brought it in."

The chest looked like the one BJ had seen in the Portland antique shop.

"Mind if I take a closer look?"

"I most certainly do mind. You can see it's there. You want anything more, you get me some papers from a judge. I gotta get back to my store now, so move along." She ushered BJ out and relocked the shed.

BJ beat a retreat back home wondering all the way why the woman was unwilling to let go of the chest without a court order. She must know Cindy was dead and she clearly was worried about a legal action, so someone, or several someones, had been trying to get ahold of it. She was expecting a fight of some kind if she let go of it to the wrong party.

She first called Baer in Portland to see if he could get her papers to release the chest. He was gone for the day and wouldn't be back until Monday. Next, she tried Lisa Carter, who was also out for the day. Frustrated, she took JD down to the beach for a long walk and some Sit/Stay practice. She was coming along—especially if BJ happened to remember a biscuit to give her as a reward.

As they walked, she thought about the chest, wondering what it contained, wondering when the sheriff was going to get it and if she could get there first.

She didn't trust Sheriff Carstairs to tell her anything, and frankly, didn't trust him to tell Lisa everything. Finally, she hit on the idea of calling Mitch Quigley. As luck would have it, he was in. She explained where the chest was, and asked him to go take a look. Mitch promised to go on his lunch hour and call her if he got any information. BJ went back to the house and paced around until the phone rang at a quarter to one.

"Hi, BJ. This is Mitch."

"Did you see the chest?"

"Wasn't able to inspect it closely, but I got a look."

"What was your impression?"

"It's a good-quality replica."

Surprised, she said, "Meaning it's not a real antique?"

"No. In fact, I doubt if it's more than a few years old."

"Isn't that odd?"

"No, there are a lot of replica works out there. They're popular."

"But not a deliberate fake?"

"Oh, no. It's a good-quality replica that doesn't pretend to be anything but a replica."

"What's it worth?"

"Between five and seven hundred."

"Okay. Thanks a lot. I appreciate you going out of your way to help me."

With regret in his tone, he said, "Whatever I can do to help you with Cindy's estate, you just let me know."

She hung up. So, the chest is not bunk, but not a museum piece. Drugs? Maybe the store and West were smuggling drugs in furniture through Hawaii, and Cindy accidentally tumbled onto it. That's why they killed her. Except, BJ reasoned, Cindy hadn't tumbled onto it. She sold the chest to the wrong man, a mistake everyone took for granted as ordinary. She bought it back and put it in storage until it could be given to West. She hadn't called the police. Nothing indicated she knew anything about any drugs or that there even were any drugs. Charlotte knew a great deal more about the irregularities in inventorying particular items, and no one had killed her.

Maybe it had nothing to do with anything.

The suspense was driving her crazy. BJ had to know about that chest—no way she could wait until Monday. She decided to go back to the shed after dark and have a closer look.

At two a.m., BJ left the house with a bag of tools and a flashlight. JD wanted to come as well. After some hesitation, she decided the dog might be helpful and brought her along. She knew she was being very fanciful to think the chest had hidden a dead body at some point, but if so, any dog would be interested in how it smelled. Besides, leaving JD alone in the house full of antiques had a downside to it.

She drove to the shop and parked off the roadway near the river and hiked back to the lot where the shops were. The place was deserted. Several lights were on at the gas station, but no one was there. The store was dark, no lights near it, and none in the parking lot. Keeping her flashlight beam shielded, she made her way to the back of the storage shed where she had seen some windows. A careful inspection of one of the windows showed it to be shut, but not locked. BJ snapped off the light and dropped it into her pocket. The window was only about three feet from the ground, so she pressed her gloved fingers against the frame around the glass and gave a hard shove upwards. With an earsplitting creak, the window raised.

Startled by the noise, BJ ducked around the side of the shed to see if anyone was in earshot. There was a house across the road and up the hill, but she couldn't see any signs of life. She wasn't sure the noise could be heard that far away. She waited for a while for any sign of activity anywhere. The night remained still.

She went back to the window, JD at her heels. The window was up far enough for her to get in. She took her light out again and played it around the interior to see if anything was up against the window. She had to reach in and move a chair so she could get access.

She climbed in and turned to JD. "Sit," she whispered. The pup reluctantly sank down. "Now stay, JD. Stay. You stay here until I can check this out."

JD responded by leaping in after her.

"Oh, great."

The pup scampered inside the shed in search of smells.

"Dog, first thing tomorrow, you go to obedience school." Slowly, BJ made her way through the piles of furniture to where the chest sat. First, she inspected it with the flashlight, going over it inch by inch. She saw nothing unusual. She felt it over carefully for anything loose or out of place. Nothing. She removed some padding around it and opened the lid. Empty, a perfectly ordinary chest. She played the flashlight over the interior carefully and felt every corner. Nothing. As a last resort, she took out a tape measure and checked the dimensions for any discrepancy.

She found one. Either the lid piece was thicker than the rest of the wood, or it wasn't solid. She tapped on the wood, and tapped on the lid. The lid had a different sound from the rest of the chest. Looking it over again, she found a miniscule indentation near the back. She got a screwdriver out of her bag and inserted it in the dent. With some effort, the interior of the lid worked loose. Between it and the exterior was some cardboard packing material. BJ pulled it out and cut it open. Inside were plastic packets of white powder. Cocaine or heroin, she surmised.

She heard the crunch of tires on gravel. Oh good, she thought, company. Just what I need. Now all I need is for that damn dog to start barking to let someone know I'm here. JD, however, was exploring some other part of the shed and oblivious to the new arrival.

Quickly, BJ put the packing back in the chest and pushed the lid in place. Someone was outside the main door with a flashlight unlocking the old door.

She thought it must be the owner. But what in hell would she be doing here at this time of night? BJ backed away from the chest and in the darkened corner down the wall from the doors, knowing she couldn't get out without making noise.

Not the owner after all. Sheriff Carstairs was who showed up. BJ could make him out clearly in the light of his car headlights as he shoved open the door and entered the shed.

The people across the road must have called when she opened the window . . . but that didn't make sense. This was Lisa's territory, and she had the night shift. Besides, if he were checking for a prowler, he would have walked around the building looking for a point of entry, not unlocked the front door. He must have used a skeleton key, she thought.

And she could tell he wasn't looking for an intruder because he immediately hastened over to the chest.

Two pieces of information clicked into place: BJ knew why he had cross-examined Bill about the chest and how he managed to afford a Rolex watch. He'd told the owner he would come next week for the chest when he got a warrant, but he never had any intention of telling a judge he wanted it.

She shifted her weight and something creaked underfoot. Carstairs swung his flashlight at her and pulled out his gun.

"Looks like you caught me in the act." BJ shoved her hands in her jacket pockets. Silently she pleaded, please arrest me, but knew she mustn't give away that she was on to him.

"Your nosy little sister told you about this, did she?"

"My sister wasn't nosy. I figured it out on my own." With a hopeful smile, she said, "Looks like I'm going back to the pen, huh?"

"What else did she tell you?" He loomed over her, and now she was getting worried. He didn't seem to be buying the act. "Aren't you supposed to let me have a lawyer before you ask questions?"

"You're not going to need a lawyer. By the time they find you, it'll be too late for a lawyer to do anything for you."

She realized she was in a lot of trouble, and suddenly BJ was filled with rage. "You killed my sister, didn't you?"

"Wasn't me. Might have been my partner. But it's just as well since she got on to all this, that bitch."

The way he said bitch, spitting it out in a tone of loud, aggressive contempt, alarmed the pup. With a savage growl, JD sprang into action. She lunged from behind the man and sunk her teeth into his calf, giving BJ the fraction of a second she needed. She didn't even take the gun out of her pocket, but swung it in Carstairs' direction and fired twice. The bullets caught him in the chest, and slammed him backwards. He went down with a groan.

Grabbing her bag off the floor, she raced for the back window, the dog right behind her. If the window hadn't awakened the neighbors, the shots would have. She was racing across the back lot toward the woods when a siren went off. Great, she thought. More cops.

Once in the woods out of sight, she slowed down to catch her breath.

First thing she had to do was get rid of the gun, then ditch her jacket with the bullet holes in it. As quietly as she could, she made her way down to the river. She heard a considerable commotion coming from the direction of the shop, but still, she never knew who might be searching, so she stepped quietly.

Probably several police cars and an ambulance would show up, she thought. She wasn't going to have much time. Hopefully, they were short-staffed and wouldn't launch a full-scale search right away.

She made it to the river and tossed the gun in. Walking farther downstream, she used the coat sleeves to tie several rocks into her jacket and tossed that in. Shivering from both cold and adrenaline, she hiked back to the car. She lost her sense of direction only once, but JD got her back on track. She was worried the police would stop her on the way home. She didn't know of any backroads into town. She'd have to drive right by the shop. She thought of leaving the car and hiking back to her home about two miles away, but if the police found her car here, it would look even worse. She could drive away from town and head up the coast, but if they had police cars coming down from up North, she could get stopped. If so, driving away from the area without a jacket at this time of night would look more suspicious than driving past the store.

She decided it was unlikely she'd be stopped, so she fired up the engine and headed down the highway. She pulled off on a side street when she heard sirens coming in her direction. She thought about stopping at a motel, but a late-night guest with a dog would be certain to rouse comment. Finally, she decided on looping around inland through the coastal range, a distance of eighty or ninety miles, and driving back home through the south side of town. That meant about three hours of driving, but it would keep her out of the way of the police.

When she finally turned down the road to Cindy's house, it was past five a.m. She half expected to see the house surrounded by police, but no one was there. Tired as she was, she knew she had things to take care of immediately. She knew glove patterns were nearly as individual as fingerprints. She had no doubt she had left imprints on the window. She had to destroy her gloves, but couldn't just throw them away. Destroying them in the fireplace would leave a residue which would look suspicious so tossing them on the fire was out. She took them into the kitchen, coated them with bacon grease, and gave them to JD to chew on. That gave her a perfectly plausible excuse for ruined gloves: the dog ate them.

Next, she knew she had to get rid of her boots. She'd probably left prints in the dust on the floor of the shed. She packaged them up for mailing using a phony return address and addressed them to the Saint Vincent de Paul store in Seattle, added what she was sure was too much postage from the stamps in Cindy's desk, then walked down to the mailbox on the corner and deposited them in the mailbox. She had two other pairs in better shape.

She stripped off the clothes she was wearing and put them in the washer and rinsed her hands and arms with ammonia cleaner that she knew would interfere with any test for gunshot residue. Finally, she was able to take a shower and fall into bed.

When she woke up again just after three in the afternoon, she got dressed and ate a snack. Despite a light drizzle falling, she took the dog for a walk to town. She wanted to buy an afternoon paper.

The blaring headline shocked BJ.

SHERIFF IMPLICATED IN DRUG SMUGGLING

That hadn't taken long.

Stunned, BJ read the account while standing on the street corner. According to the article, a search of Carstairs's pockets revealed evidence against him and Kilpper. A search of Kilpper's home the night before turned up more drugs hidden in furniture purchased through the store along with evidence of payoffs to the sheriff.

Realizing she was drawing attention to herself by reading the paper in the rain, she tucked it under her arm and walked back home. She reread the article three times before it all sunk in. This raised more questions for her than it answered. Who shot Kilpper? Velda? Or his partner in crime, Carstairs?

With Kilpper dead, who did they suspect shot the sheriff? And was Carstairs telling the truth when he said he hadn't killed Cindy but his partner might have? Most importantly, did anyone suspect her?

The news article said nothing about any suspects. She decided the best thing she could do was to keep a low profile for a few days and stay at home.

She got a phone call on the landline later that evening.

"Is this BJ McKay, Cindy's sister?" an unfamiliar woman's voice asked.

"Yeah. What can I do for you?"

"This is Lucy."

"Lucy?"

"Lucy Kaufman."

"Lucy Kaufman? Oh yeah. Yeah. The antique dealer who handles Russian stuff."

"You know I tried to get ahold of your sister, but the line was out of order. I finally sent a registered letter, but then I had to leave for Europe."

"I thought you went to Georgia."

"Yes. Georgia, the *country*, not the state, and then I went on to Saint Petersburg."

"What about Alaska?"

"That was more recently. I just returned yesterday."

"Just curious, why send a note registered?" BJ asked.

"To make sure Cindy got it. I wasn't going to be available while out of the country, and it was important."

"I see. Do you know anything about a gold coin and this egg Cindy bought?"

"Yes, I have them both."

"Could you drop them in the post for me?"

"Drop them in the post? You'd better come up here."

"Oh. Well. All right. I'll be up in a few days, not sure when, if that's okay."

"I'll see you when you can manage. I just found out about Cindy. I didn't know until yesterday that she was dead. I've been in and out of town a lot or I would have said something earlier. I'm so shocked."

By Tuesday, BJ felt restless. The local newspaper reported connections the city police made between Edward West, Gerry Ranson, Steven Kilpper, and the sheriff in their scheme to import drugs into the country from Turkey through Hawaii hidden in replica antiques. Nothing was mentioned about a suspect in the sheriff's death.

BJ strolled down the street with all the antique shops, not having any idea what she might learn. She stopped in to see Mitch, but he wasn't working. She noticed that Bingham's was closed down and sealed off with yellow crime scene tape. Presumably law enforcement was busily examining all the furniture for more drug stashes. Idly, she walked around behind the store to revisit the place where they'd found Kilpper's body. A lot of cars were parked in back, but otherwise the place seemed oddly deserted. No shoppers here. BJ stared at the spot where she and Kate had found the body.

"You're one of them, too, aren't you?" asked a soft quiet voice behind her.

BJ spun around to find herself less than six feet away from Velda Cox. Velda glared at her intently, her eyes oddly dilated. With both hands, she gripped an over-sized brown leather purse in front of her, as if about ready to reach in.

"No, I'm not one of them," BJ contradicted, not sure what else to say. She wondered if she could reach Velda and grab her before she got a gun out of her purse. She was too far away at the moment. Cautiously, BJ took a step forward.

Velda nimbly retreated several steps. "No, that won't work. You can't catch me."

"I don't want to catch you. I want to leave. I'm from out of town. I have nothing to do with you."

"Yes, you DO! You stole money from me—you and that fancy lawyer of yours."

"Hardly fancy," BJ said, not knowing what else to say.

"You're trying to put me out of business."

"No, I'm not. I'm not in the antique business. I have no interest in your business."

"You're doing it for your sister."

"My sister is dead."

"Serves her right, too."

"The sheriff killed her," BJ said, wondering if Velda would contradict that assertion and make a confession.

"He was a bastard. He wouldn't help me. I told him and told him, but he wouldn't help me. Now he's dead, too." She opened her purse and started to reach inside.

"Freeze! Police!"

BJ looked to the left and saw Detective Lisa Carter partially hidden behind a pile of pallets and holding her gun in a shooter's stance.

Velda also turned in Lisa's direction. With a screech, she reached to pull something out of her purse.

BJ heard a gunshot.

Velda's mouth opened as if she were trying to say something. She listed to the side, closed her eyes, and crumpled to a heap.

"Holy shit!" BJ said.

Lisa didn't speak. She kept the gun out in front of her and approached Velda. When she reached the body, she kicked the handbag out of reach and handcuffed the motionless figure.

BJ took a few steps closer. Lisa opened Velda's bag and, much to BJ's surprise, revealed a large kitchen knife.

No gun.

BJ spent a couple of hours at the cop shop giving her statement and thought she was done with it. But later that evening, she got a call from Lisa, who sounded coldly official, asking her to come over to Velda's property to identify some items that might possibly have belonged to Cindy. BJ jotted down the address and directions and was told to walk around the house to the old barn in back.

Darkness had settled all around, but the area outside the old barn was lit up with portable spotlights. At least a dozen vehicles were scattered about including a forensic van in the driveway. They must have found a shitload of evidence, BJ thought, parking her car and walking to the barn.

She stepped inside and gasped. Lights everywhere inside the barn lit up every corner. A dozen people in uniforms busied themselves with various tasks, including a photographer whose flash pops added a syncopated brilliance to the interior. These were not what took BJ's breath away.

Directly across from the double door entrance, BJ saw life-sized card board cut-outs of people. The bodies were those of Star Wars imperial soldiers and Star Trek figures with some real clothes draped on them, but the heads had full sized photographs pasted onto them, those of Cindy, Kilpper, Marsh, Mitch, Charlotte, two men BJ did not recognize, and Sheriff Carstairs. The faces of Cindy, Kilpper and Carstairs had thick black crosses drawn across them. They also had targets drawn on their torsos, and all had bullet holes puncturing the cut outs.

BJ stood rooted to the spot, staring, until Lisa came up to her and said, "Could you take a look at that blouse on the figure of your sister and tell me if you recognize it?

BJ nodded and walked over to the figures. The blouse, a white lace one stapled to the figure, was shot full of holes. She shook her head. "I can't tell you if that's Cindy's or not. It's her style and her size, but it looks relatively new. It's not something I remember seeing her wear."

To BJ's left, she saw a work bench running nearly the length of the barn loaded with what looked like parts of dolls. She took a few steps closer to get a better look. Lisa did not try to stop her.

"Oh, my God," BJ whispered.

"Yeah," Lisa said gently. "If you have any guilty feelings about Velda being shot on your behalf, you can lose them. She was a very sick person."

On the workbench were figures of Ken and Barbie dolls in various torture apparatus including a guillotine cutting off Barbie's head, stocks imprisoning Ken, who had a metal cage clamped on his head. Another Barbie was cramped inside a cage with her limbs sticking out. A second Ken was attached to a rack with his limbs being pulled apart.

Interspersed with the Ken and Barbie dolls were other toys, model horses ripping Ken apart, a model car running over a tied-up Barbie. All the Ken and Barbie figures were naked, their genitals and nipples painted red. BJ looked over the work bench and counted. Thirty-seven different torture and murder scenarios.

BJ said, "All this must have taken a while."

"Months at least," Lisa said.

Above the work bench was a punch board for holding tools. Affixed to it were saws, knives, a machete, a fireplace poker, horse hobbles, chains, handcuffs, and a few other items BJ could not identify.

"Find any guns?" BJ asked.

"Lots, including three thirty-eights. We'll see if any of them match the gun or guns that killed Kilpper and Carstairs."

"Need me for anything else?"

"No. You can go home now."

"Thanks."

"I'd suggest you try to get this out of your mind. A drink might help."

"A drink? I'm gonna need a whole fucking bottle."

CHAPTER TEN

Closed Files

Two weeks later, Lisa, Vicky, Mary, Kate, and BJ were again having tea.

Once they were all settled and cheerfully ensconced in front of the fire buttering scones and sipping *Lapsang Souchong*, Lisa launched into her report of the recent decisions made by the chief of police.

"As far as the chief is concerned, he has closed out all four murders, and they are considered solved." Lisa announced.

"He made Velda for Cindy's murder?" BJ asked, wondering if something definitive had been found in the bar.

"We know Velda put Cindy on her hate list from what we found in her barn, specifically, the large cut-out with Cindy's face on it and the X-mark through it."

Mary shook her head. "I have a hard time seeing someone as old as Velda managing to strangle a healthy young woman. You think it's possible?"

"As far as the evidence shows, yes. The theory is that Velda used some pretext to get Cindy to drive the both of them down to the area where the body was found. Once Cindy stopped the car, Velda, who was likely seated directly in back of her, garroted Cindy with a length of rope."

BJ said, "The newspaper said Cindy died of strangulation. I assumed that meant some man's hands." She hated thinking about what her sister went through.

"The medical examiner allowed the newspaper to print death by strangulation, but kept it secret that Cindy was garroted, not manually strangled." Picking up on BJ's distress, Lisa said, "I'm sorry to talk about your sister this way."

BJ nodded silently, trying not to shed tears.

Kate said, "Even a petite, elderly woman could have pulled the body out of the car and driven off in it."

"Yes," Lisa said. "Velda ditched the car by driving through the gap in the fence at the junk yard and smashed out the windows to make it look like a wreck. She could have parked her own car in the vicinity in a number of places within easy walking distance where it would have been out of sight."

BJ was having a hard time following Velda's motivations. And then did Velda use Cindy's keys to get into the house—looking for what? BJ couldn't make sense of that.

"Did you find Cindy's keys in Velda's possession?" BJ asked.

Lisa shook her head. "No. Nothing that directly links her to your sister's murder."

Mary raised her hand, a perplexed look on her face. "How does the chief explain the fact that nearly a whole year went by before Velda went after anyone else on her hate list?"

"His theory is that Velda was so afraid of getting caught, she didn't try anything for months. She was waiting to see where the investigation went. When Edward West was murdered, she got active again."

Kate said, "He's not making her for West's murder, is he?"

"No. That is being attributed to West's involvement with drugs. With some help from the FBI, what we've been able to put together is that Omar Smith in Turkey shipped heroin to the shop owned by West in Hawaii where it was packed into replica antique pieces which were shipped here, turned over to West, and he and Gerry Ranson distributed in Seattle. They did it this roundabout way to hide West's involvement. Someone in Hawaii might have noticed if odd pieces of furniture were going to his place in Seattle.

"Somewhere along the line," Lisa said, "Carstairs found out, so he was getting paid off."

Mary said, "The paper said something about evidence in Carstairs's pocket?"

Lisa said, "A ledger containing a list of pieces of furniture shipped from Hawaii to the shop here in town along with a notation of the dates and the values of the drugs. We assume the values listed were for the drugs, because they far exceeded the price of the furniture. Looks like they smuggled nearly a million dollars of heroin into the country."

"Sounds like enough to be worth killing for."

"The ledger was in Kilpper's handwriting. We searched his home, and in his back shed found some of the furniture. My theory is they were emptied of their contents and the drugs turned over to West, who also sometimes took whatever pieces of furniture the drugs were in back to Seattle, depending on the size and how easy it would be to transport. We found secret compartments and traces of heroin in all of them."

"So who killed West?" BJ asked.

"Kilpper. Or that's the official theory. We don't actually know. It is assumed that when the sea chest went missing, West got suspicious that maybe he'd been double-crossed. He came down here to straighten things out with Kilpper, who panicked and killed him."

"But they'd been drinking together," Kate pointed out. "West thinks Kilpper double-crossed him so he lets Kilpper drink him under the table? That doesn't sound likely."

Vicky said, "A better theory would be that Carstairs realized that with the chest missing, the whole conspiracy was unraveling, and he killed West. Only because the deputy sheriff was in a car accident while on the way there did the police, not his department, end up investigating that murder."

"Oh yeah," BJ said. "I had forgotten about that. Carstairs must have been completely freaked out that he didn't have control."

"If Carstairs had been in charge," Vicky said, "he could have easily manipulated the investigation so someone else was framed, or it went nowhere. Kilpper has lived next to the ocean for ages. He wouldn't be stupid enough to put a body in the water when he knew the tide would wash it up. Not to mention the fact that Carstairs was big and strong, and it would have been easier for him than Kilpper to carry the body of a man out to the end of the pier."

Lisa pressed her lips together. In an odd voice, she said, "The chief has attributed the murder to Kilpper."

Mary said, "Oh, I get it. He doesn't want to give law enforcement a black eye."

Lisa looked away. "Kilpper or Carstairs, either way, it's not like we have a killer still on the loose."

Oh, don't you? BJ thought.

Vicky piped up and said, "How do you hook up Kilpper with West's murder?"

"Lots of things. In his home safe, Carstairs had twenty-thousand in cash in new bills that we've traced to a bank in Seattle that gave them to West. The bills have Kilpper's fingerprints on them. We assume Carstairs took them into evidence and had them in his home for safekeeping. We also found some packets of heroin in Kilpper's home safe with West's fingerprints on them. The theory is that once West was drunk, he was drowned in the bathtub and taken out a back door near his room and thrown into the ocean from there."

BJ heard what Lisa wasn't saying—that Kilpper didn't kill West, Carstairs did. She decided not to make an issue of it. It didn't affect her one way or the other.

"The hotel's back door isn't alarmed?" Vicky asked.

"No. You have to have a key to open it from either side, but no alarm goes off."

"Is Carstairs involvement in the drug conspiracy pretty solid?" Vicky asked.

"I took a look at Carstairs' home," Lisa said. "He's got a stereo system and media center worth about ten thousand dollars and a computer worth thousands. He's got gold and diamond jewelry in his bedroom worth a fortune. He has a collection of antique revolvers worth tens of thousands of dollars and a Lotus sportscar in the garage. After you made that remark about his watch, I asked around, and he did not come into any money as far as anyone knew. Also, since he was killed, I checked with the IRS, and he's never reported anything but his sheriff's salary for the last twenty-five years."

"So Velda killed Kilpper and Carstairs?" Mary asked her.

"The theory is that the murder of Edward West got her active again, somehow. Her sister, Theodora, says Velda has spent a lot more time in the last year back in the barn, so the chief thinks that's how she was handling her anger until recently."

"Is there physical evidence connecting the deaths?" Kate asked.

"There's what we found in the barn which indicates a deep resentment of Cindy, Kilpper, and Carstairs, with others, and a very disturbed personality. Also, Velda inherited a bunch of guns from her husband. We have a list from his insurance company, and it includes five different thirty-eight revolvers, six Glock semi-automatic nine-millimeters, a four-shot thirty-two revolver, five High Standard twenty-two caliber target pistols, a SIG Sauer, and some others I'm not remembering off the top of my head. We haven't found all the guns on the list. A bunch, including five thirty-eights, are missing."

"Do the ballistics match up?" Mary asked.

"No. None of the thirty-eights we found matched up with the gun that killed Kilpper or Carstairs. They don't match up with each other, by the way. Two different guns were used. We think after Velda shot Kilpper, she tossed the gun into the ocean. After shooting Carstairs, she threw the second gun into the river. That would be the smart thing to do. No one is going to find a gun in that river. It flows too fast and has too many rapids.

Glad you approve, BJ thought.

Kate said, "Bit of a change in modus operandi from strangulation to shooting."

"Easily explained. Velda could kill a small woman with a garrote when she was an unsuspecting car driver, but it would have been nearly impossible for Velda to kill two large men that way—and less likely she could lure them into a vulnerable position after her repeated outbursts of rage."

"But no solid physical evidence," Mary asked, "just the figures in the barn and her confrontations?"

BJ tensed and tried not to say out loud what was running through her head: Shut up, Mary. Leave it alone. Don't get Lisa thinking.

"We did find some tire tracks on the roadside not far from where Carstairs was shot and believe they were made not long before or after the shooting, based on the rain. They were consistent with a compact, like the one Velda drives, but not clear enough to make an exact match."

Mary kept on talking and BJ wanted to clobber her. "Did anyone check Carstairs' gun to see if that was the one that shot Kilpper? If Carstairs killed West to cover up the drug trafficking before the operation fell apart, he would want to kill Kilpper as well, and Velda's accusations gave him the perfect cover."

"According to the chief, since we *know* Velda killed both those men, there's no point in wasting time or money doing any such tests as you have described," Lisa said in an official tone, clearly imitating her boss.

Vicky said, "And I had my money on Towerson."

"Why, what's he been doing?" Lisa asked.

"Staying at the Embarcadero," Vicky said, "without his family. I talked to my friend who works there, and she checked the hotel register. He's been down a dozen times in the last several years. She also tells me there's a rumor that he has female companionship while he's here."

Kate asked, "Didn't Velda's sister know what was going on?"

"That's complicated," Lisa said. "Yes, she knew Velda was having mental problems but she claims she had no idea they were this bad."

"But wasn't Velda on medication?" BJ asked, remembering the woman's flat affect while talking to her at the tea shop.

"The story I've discovered is that Velda would absolutely not see a psychiatrist," Lisa said. "When she went in to see her GP, he'd prescribe anti-psychotic medication, but he refused to authorize refills without a re-examination, and Theodora could only get Velda to go in when Velda had some other problem, like flu, or shingles, or once a broken arm. When things got bad, she would drug Velda with cold medication, but Velda built up a tolerance level, then got her own doctor to prescribe tranquillizers and she was slipping those into Velda's food when Velda had bad days."

"Sounds like this was going on for quite a while," Vicky said.

"Years," Lisa said. "In fact, we're now wondering if the death of Velda's husband thirteen years ago might have been more than it seemed. He died of intestinal problems. His doctor put it down to natural causes since he was an old man, but no autopsy was done. Now those of us at the station house are wondering if Velda might have poisoned him. The experts we've consulted tell us Velda's condition is one that developed over a long period of time. She didn't suddenly become a homicidal maniac."

"And Theodora never tried to get her institutionalized?" Mary asked.

"She says she didn't think Velda was dangerous."

"What was going on in the shed didn't worry her?" BJ asked, incredulous.

"She says she never went into it," Lisa replied.

"And do you believe her?" Kate asked.

"No."

Mary said, "I'll bet there's money in it somewhere."

"Good guess. The shop the women owned doesn't make a lot of money. They both collect social security, but the biggest source of income they had was the pension from Velda's husband as his widow."

Mary said, "And if Velda was institutionalized, her sister no longer gets that money."

"That's right."

"Pity you can't charge her with some sort of crime," Mary said.

"Or Velda's doctor. He knew Velda needed to be hospitalized," Lisa said angrily, "and he's known it for years, but didn't want to stick his neck out."

"I wonder why we keep referring to Velda as insane," Kate pondered, "rather than plain evil."

"I am going to leave that discussion to theologians," Lisa said.

"So am I," BJ said with a smile. "If you all will excuse me, I'd better get home to a pup who is probably chewing up the house by now."

"I'll go out with you," Kate said.

They walked slowly out to the cars together, BJ lost in thought.

Kate said, "I haven't seen much of you lately."

"Yeah, sorry about that. Been pretty busy."

"I suppose you're probably still a bit in shock after all that with Velda."

"Yeah, guess so."

"Hope you'll come by the café again soon."

"I'll try," BJ said, trying to sound casual.

Kate stood a moment as they reached BJ s car, then somewhat reluctantly, walked on by to her own car. BJ knew Kate was disappointed not to get more of a response from her. She sighed, reached a hand to her inner pocket and touched a letter.

Susan had written her. She was back in the United States, staying in California. She'd sent the letter in care of BJ's court-appointed attorney who had forwarded it to Brian Baer, who had sent it to BJ in Ocean City. Susan wanted to see her again.

The letter had sent BJ into shock. She had no idea what she felt. Of course, she wanted things to be the way they had been before Patrick had shown up at the door, but eight years and a murder trial later, she knew they would not be able to just pick up where they'd left off. For all she knew, Susan was in a new relationship. The letter was cryptic. "I'm in the country again, need to see you."

On the one hand, BJ wanted to get on with her life as it was; on the other, she felt she needed to at least see if resuming a relationship with Susan was possible. She didn't feel she could explain this to Kate right now. It might complicate things unnecessarily if BJ found out Susan was in a new relationship.

BJ got in her car to drive back to Cindy's house on Pine Street. She still thought of it as Cindy's house. She didn't consider herself to be living there, only staying there. Could she and Susan pick up where they'd left off? Their relationship had ended over eight years ago when she'd shot Patrick Hunter through a door.

And if she were honest, her action was not really in self-defense, not like it had been with the sheriff.

She hadn't been afraid Patrick would come in and shoot her. She was afraid he would go away and catch one of them with their guard down, and she was tired of worrying about when that might be, so she shot to kill. Afterwards, she vowed whatever happened to her later in life, she would never, never, ever, shoot another cop.

But with Carstairs she really had acted in self-defense. Her life was at risk that night. She was sure he killed West and Kilpper when their enterprise showed signs of tanking, using Velda's insanity as a cover, and he would no doubt have killed her that night but for the dog.

With all that running through her mind, she realized she needed to see what she and Susan might have left before she could pursue anyone else. She was sorry to disappoint Kate, but she still had remnants of her old life to square away.

CHAPTER ELEVEN

The Egg

There are things that you can't walk away from.

That was the text BJ had gotten from Susan. Once connected, they had exchanged emails and talked on the phone, but so much could not be said in a phone call, much less in an email. Still, Susan had felt it necessary to send BJ that text on why she was back in the States.

There are things you can't walk away from.

After she shot Patrick, BJ had sat down on the front porch and waited for the police. It hadn't occurred to her to try to run away. She felt very differently about her current shooting of Sheriff Carstairs. She felt as if she'd walked into the middle of a play, in a second act she wasn't supposed to be in, so she made a quick, necessary, exit. She was not supposed to have been in the story of the drug smuggling at all, not any more than Cindy was supposed to have been involved. But unlike the death of Patrick, the death of Carstairs was resolved. Law enforcement was satisfied. The file was closed.

Her life resumed. She was having her leatherworking tools shipped down to Ocean Side, her new home. She had decided to live on the coast permanently. She and Susan had arranged to meet in a few weeks. Susan was currently in Los Angeles and her older sister was going to go into the hospital for heart surgery, so Susan would be coming up to Portland later, and they would see each other again.

BJ started to pick up the pieces of her life. She bought a new laptop and started recreating her client list, sending off emails to drum up new work projects. She called Kate and explained about Susan, and they agreed to get together after BJ and Susan met in Portland. BJ wanted to get closure on that relationship, because of course she did realize they wouldn't be picking up where they left off with eight years and the dead body of an ex-husband between them.

Still, *there are things you can't walk away from.*

On an afternoon the week following the killing of Sheriff Carstairs, BJ invited Sallie Wald over for afternoon tea. She poured several pots of homemade herbal tea, which they drank with a selection of tea sandwiches, cakes, and cheeses. They chatted amiably about the weather and books and dogs.

Finally, after Sallie drained her sixth cup of tea, BJ got around to the point. After that much tea, she was starting to feel woozy and knew she needed to finish this.

"I thought you might want to know that I found this," BJ said, taking a jewel-encrusted egg out of a box that had been sitting on a buffet behind her.

"Ah . . . the Ukrainian Easter egg," Sallie said with a nod.

BJ thought Sallie's eyes appeared out of focus, but that might have been her imagination. Were Sallie's words becoming slightly slurred? Or was that also BJ's imagination?

"That's not a Ukrainian Easter egg and you know it." BJ handed Sallie a copy of the letter Lucy had sent to Cindy.

"I knew it! I knew it," Sallie shrieked. "And that idiot landlord sold it to Cindy for five dollars! Five dollars! All because she got into the estate sale ahead of everyone else."

"Lucy got it appraised. One like this sold to the Metropolitan Museum of Art for two-and-a-half million dollars. That's hardly more than the value of the jewels on it. After Cindy got it, you tried to break in and steal it from her, even cutting the phone cord to keep her from finding out what she had. When that didn't work, you killed her and used her keys to get in, but couldn't find it. She'd already sent it off to Lucy by then along with the 1899 ten-ruble gold coin."

Sallie shook her head. "I'm an old frail lady with a heart condition. Your sister was young and healthy. How could I have killed her?"

"With a few good lies. All you had to do was come up with some pretext for needing Cindy to drive you down to a deserted area near the beach early in the morning, and then also come up with a pretext for needing to ride in the back seat of her car. Maybe you told her that you needed to stretch your leg out along the back, maybe you said you were used to riding in back. Why would she argue?

Once parked down in the dunes by the old warehouse, Cindy stopped the car, and you garroted her from the back seat. You'd need very little strength to choke her to death if you caught her by surprise. Then, you pulled her body out of the front seat, got in, and drove the car to the junkyard. You drove through the gap between the fence and the cliffside in back and smashed out some windows to make it look like a wreck. After that, you walked to your own car, which you'd parked nearby. Then all you had to do was find the egg."

Sallie sat, arms folded over her chest, and rolled her eyes. "I won't dignify that with a response."

"You broke in here again when I told you I would be away."

Sallie sat back in her chair and smirked. "You won't ever prove any of that, you know. Velda did it as far as everyone is concerned, and now the case is closed. You have no evidence against me."

BJ noticed when Sallie's hands dropped limply into her lap. She also noticed that the room was tilting. Not long now.

"But you killed her, didn't you? You thought only Cindy knew about the egg. You could even claim Cindy gave it to you for the library and just figure I wouldn't know any better."

Sallie leaned forward. Starting to sound a little bit drunk, she drawled, "If you've got a tape-recorder and are hoping for a confession, you're going to be dish-dish-appointed. You can't prove any of that. Whoever killed Cindy was an experienced criminal, one who knew how to hide the car, eliminate all traces of crime."

"You didn't need prior experience to do that. You probably read about it in a book. Good mystery fiction has lots of tips about getting away with murder."

"Even if all that is true, there's . . . nuff-nuffing you can do about it now." Sallie smirked some more, but her eyes were definitely losing focus, and her words were perceptively slurred.

The smirk relieved BJ of any feelings of guilt. This woman had murdered her lovely young sister and here she was *smirking* about it. BJ hadn't thought she'd feel guilty. She wasn't about Sheriff Carstairs, but she'd had no option but to kill him in self-defense. She hadn't been sure how she would feel about this meeting with Sallie, but *there were things you didn't walk away from.*

"On the contrary," BJ said. "Not only *can* I do something about it, I already have. There's more than mint in this herbal tea. It's mixed with foxglove. Apparently, I got the foxglove confused with comfrey. It's a common amateur's mistake. There's nothing wrong with *my* heart. I can survive a massive dose of digitalis. But you, on the other hand, are a different story, if you'll pardon the expression. If I'd noticed this mistake a little sooner, I could have called 9-1-1 and with induced vomiting, we would have both survived. Looks like it's a little late for that now. Thank you for not saying anything to cause me to have any doubts. I didn't really, but I had to leave a window of opportunity to change the results. Just in case."

Sallie tried to stand, but she didn't make it to her feet. BJ waited until she was quite sure Sallie was dead and then called 911.

Semper Fi.

About The Author

Award-winning crime and mystery author, Deni Starr, practiced law in Portland, Oregon, for fifteen years, handling criminal cases, family law matters, and personal injury cases. Additionally, she's worked as a freelance private investigator and managed criminal investigation for her law practice.

Starr has three mainstream books in publication, *Below the Belt, Sucker-Punched,* and *Throwing in the Towel,* all contemporary crime drama mysteries set in Portland with a fighting arts theme. Her fourth book in that series, *Saved by the Bell,* will be published in February 2020. For more information, please visit the author's website:

www.DeniStarrMysteries.com